Prisoners

Out of the Box, Book 10

Robert J. Crane

Prisoners
Out of the Box #10
Robert J. Crane
Copyright © 2016 Revelen Press
All Rights Reserved.

1st Edition

1.

There are two types of people in the world.

In the days of yore, when we used to hang people from a gallows for wrongdoing, the first type would see that criminal swinging, tongue sticking out, face turning blue, and say, "Gosh, I don't ever want that to happen to me." Then they'd go live their life, taking particular care to avoid thieving, murdering, or generally causing harm.

The second type would take in that same scene, with that same dead body, face distorted in fear and agony, and think, "That'll never happen to me." And then they'd go on about their life, thieving, murdering, and harming anyone who got in their way.

I hate that second type.

But then again, that second type was how I had made my livelihood since the day I'd left my house for the first time. Beating the ass of metahumans who got out of line and tossing them in the stir was my bread and butter—or at least how I paid for my bread and butter. And honey, because bread and butter on its own just isn't my jam.

Oh, and it's how I pay for my jam. Because you can't eat bread and butter and honey all the time.

My bread and butter and honey and jam and money were the reason I found myself hanging out the door of a helicopter over Portland, Oregon, at three o'clock in the morning when I damned well ought to have been back in my own bed. Instead, I was staring down at a four-story office building that was slightly pyramidal, as though the architect

1

had decided upright walls were just a little too passé for his hipster soul.

"Nice sign they left out for us," my brother, Reed, said from beside me. He was a big-ish guy, which is to say bigger than me. He was hovering just over my shoulder as I chewed my lip and looked down at this unnatural monstrosity of suburban sprawl. It was made somewhat more unnatural by a hard casing of ice that covered every single window on the first floor of the building. It looked like a glacier had run into the building and just slid around it, freezing again once it had it good and surrounded.

It was September. In Portland. The grass was green, the night cool but still at least twenty degrees above freezing, so a building with the whole ground floor encased in ice? Not normal.

"Yo, this ice is thick," Augustus Coleman's voice crackled in my earpiece over the wash of the chopper's blades. "We're talking three, four feet at least."

"And it's cold, too," Kat Forrest piped up in my ear. I controlled the roll of my eyes to prevent injury. "Brrrrr!"

"Yes, ice is cold," I deadpanned as I surveyed the building below. It was called Palleton Labs, some local concern. The ice had formed several hours ago, when the gang and I had just so happened to be in Fresno, wrapping up a local meta criminal for handover to the feds. He'd been robbing banks, battering his way into the vaults late at night and walking off with tons of cash. He wasn't a hard guy to find, with his brand new Lamborghini parked out in front of his tenement building. When we took him down, I counted over a hundred pieces of diamond jewelry the guy had just lying out on his table, plus an eighty-inch 4k HD TV. He also had a brand new jet ski under his carport.

I had a feeling that whoever was lingering in Palleton Labs was probably not quite as dumb as our last quarry. But then, that was a low bar to clear.

"What do you figure?" Reed asked, somehow coming off like a rural sheriff in his delivery.

"I figure we bust in and bust heads," I said, giving him some well-deserved side-eye.

"So, the usual, then?" Augustus offered. I could see him far below as our PD chopper circled, a shadow lurking outside the frozen barrier.

"Start breaking the ice," I said. "Reed and I will meet you inside."

"Oh, man," Augustus said. "Hey, Kat, any chance you wanna—"

I heard what I thought was a rustle in the breeze at first, the trees below shaking, visible even by the dim light of the fluorescent streetlamps. Then I saw boughs whipping along the side of Palleton Labs, slapping hard at the ice barriers on the side windows.

"Yeah," Augustus said lamely. "Like that."

"We get to jump?" Reed asked, and I caught a hint of reticence from him.

I gave him a sweet smile. "You get to jump. I can fly." And I left him behind, shooting out the door toward the roof of the labs.

"You are such a pain in the ass," Reed grumbled, and then I heard the wind whip in his microphone as he jumped out of the chopper. The wind shifted directions behind me, coming hard out of the north. I shivered as I drew closer to the tar and gravel roof below, then touched down as gently as if I were taking a simple step off a staircase.

Reed thumped to a landing behind me, blowing up the tail of my jacket as he came down. It was like standing next to a helicopter as it landed, and my hair flew all over my face. I spat a long strand out of my mouth and rearranged it back behind my ear. "Remind me to wear a ponytail next time I fly with you."

"That was barely a flight," he scoffed. He was wearing a leather jacket, too. Not because we'd needed them in Cali, but because they looked cool.

"Then why were you such a baby about it before we jumped?" I asked, looking around for a roof door. It didn't look like I was going to find one.

"Because I can't always control my landings," he said, sweeping left and right over the bare roof, launching off the metal ducting in a stir of wind and coming to a landing on

3

the far side of the roof. "No entry over here."

"Bummer," I said, shrugging as I made my way over to the far corner of the building. "I need your help here for a sec."

He flew up and over in a low arc about ten feet off the roof and came down, a little more gently this time. "What did you say? I don't think I heard you."

"I said come help me, dick."

"What do you need help with, oh great and mighty?" he asked, smirking in the darkness.

"Something pretty minimal, and thus perfect for you," I said, listening to the sound of trees battering against ice somewhere below. "I'm going to cut through the roof—"

"With what?" Augustus chirped from below. I could hear the boredom in his voice. Watching trees beat the shit out of an icy barricade had apparently lost its excitement already.

"With fire, of course," I said, lightning up a finger with Gavrikov's power. "Blowtorch style."

"And you're not going to burn the place down?" Kat asked, sounding like she was both mildly concerned and mildly exerting herself controlling the trees.

"I control fire, fools," I said. "Now, Reed, get ready to vortex the roof section I cut off so it doesn't go crashing down and warn them we're coming."

"Because the sound of trees hammering at their barricade isn't warning enough?" Reed asked.

"Well, they may know that Kat and Augustus are coming, but that doesn't mean we need to ruin the element of surprise for ourselves," I said, kneeling down and sticking my blowtorch finger into the tar ceiling. I made it a very focused flame, cutting right through the roof and pulling it in a slow circle.

"Wait, we're the distraction?" Augustus sounded a little nonplussed. "Like ... sacrificial lambs? Because I'm guessing the thing that did this was a frost giant. You know, a Jotun."

"Don't be all dramatic about it," I said, about halfway done with my cutting job. "Most frost giants are the size of normal people, and the only one I met who wasn't was a total wuss who still had to get other people to fight his battles for him. Besides, we don't even know what we're

4

dealing with. You could be two-on-one against some frost dwarf."

"Man, I don't want to fight Iceman Peter Dinklage," Augustus said.

"Peter Dinklage was Bolivar Trask, not Bobby Drake," Reed said idly, his attention on the hole I was nearly done carving in the roof. His hand was shaking slightly, and I could hear a gust pushing on the segment of roof I'd cut out, whistling through the ceiling and ductwork within. It rattled and then popped out the little circle of roof, and carried it about five feet away before setting it gently upon the tar and gravel.

I poked my head into the hole, and there was nothing but darkness. "Lumos!" I said for fun, and the fire on my fingertips sprang up. I stuck my hand in the hole and saw ceiling tiles below, along with some wiring and other stuff. I reached for the ceiling tile separating me from whatever was below and failed, my height once again holding me back. "Reed," I said, "be a good sport and get this tile, would you?"

He was leaning over me, looking down. "It's not gonna be that quiet. I suspect that last gust probably rattled through the ducts."

"Over the sound of the Entish army below, who's going to notice wind in the ceiling?" I asked, mostly joking to cover my worry. This was not quiet so far, not nearly so quiet as if I'd had a damned door in the roof I could've just broken and entered.

"Any meta with half decent hearing," Reed said as he blew the ceiling tile up and out of the hole in the roof. I barely moved my head out of the way in time.

"Great," I grumbled as I dropped down into Palleton Labs, fluorescent lighting giving me a clear picture of a white tile floor waiting beneath me. It smelled like a hospital, sort of sterile. The wall was beige but with a subtle crosshatching pattern that suggested wallpaper rather than paint. There were office doors and windows behind me, lining the outer perimeter of the building, and a solid wall to my right that suggested there was a central room or series of rooms on this level that was a little more hidden from public view.

I cleared my entry hole and Reed came in behind me, messing up my hair once more. "Okay, seriously?" I said, spitting out a strand again.

"Isabella carries a hair tie on her wrist," Reed said, a little too proud of himself. "You know, for just such occasions."

"She also carries a six-foot iron pole up her rectum," I said, "and your balls in her purse. But you don't see me doing either one of those things." I lifted off the ground and hovered my way toward the corner ahead like a specter.

"Harsh," Augustus said.

"Are you going to bust down the damned ice anytime soon or are you gonna let the little blond girl do all the work for you, Augustus?" I sniped.

There was a second's pause. "I guess I kinda asked for that, but … yeah, let me mess up the landscaping here and we'll be along shortish." I heard a sound like earth moving, and I knew that he was finally taking a hand in busting through the ice. I liked Augustus a lot, but I was pretty sure sometimes he forgot exactly how much power he had at his fingertips. I hadn't told him, but he was without doubt the strongest meta on the team other than myself. I didn't want him to get a swelled head, but the day he decided to start using his powers to the fullest instead of holding back for fear of hurting someone, he was going to be a force to be reckoned with.

The sound of our teammates railing against the ice got louder, floating up from floors below, and I listened for anything closer than that. I was rewarded with the squeak of Reed's shoe against the tile floor, and I froze, my irritation rising.

"Sorry," he said, probably able to read my frustration in my body posture, "I wasn't expecting an op right now."

"Always expect an op," I said, starting forward again. "It's not the Spanish Inquisition."

"Heh," he said under his breath, so low it was a whisper of a whisper, audible only to meta ears up close.

The sound of trees and now something else—Augustus in armor—whaling on the side of the building provided a disquieting soundtrack to our forward creep. I was moving slowly so as not to abandon Reed. I cast frequent looks back as he crept along, trying to avoid squeaking as we approached the corner. The sound of boughs on ice reverberating through the building reminded me of a movie where they turned up the noise of a drum in the background, thumping every few seconds as the tension built to a fever pitch.

I waited at the corner as Reed crept up behind me, barely breathing. "You look tense," he said as I stuck my head out. Down the corridor, light filtered out from a door to the center of the building in a thin shaft. It looked misshapen, like someone had busted through it.

"I am not all about that bass right now," I said as the sound of thumping grew even louder, more unnerving, more irritating. It should have been a soothing sound, that of help being on the way, but instead it was grating. They were hammering so hard that I could feel the shuddering of the building all around me.

"I figured you'd be a huge fan of that song," Reed said, and I didn't have to turn around to hear the glee in his words.

I started to reply with a barb of my own, but something broke far below us, making a shattering noise that echoed up through the hall. "We're in," Augustus said, huffing a little.

"*You're* in," Kat said, doing a little huffing of her own, "I'm still behind you. Wait up, will you?"

"I will n—*oh, shit!*" Augustus shouted.

The building shook again, something smashing into something else. I shot an alarmed look at Reed. Kat chimed in just in time: "We have met the enemy, and he is not a frost Peter Dinklage! He's *big*, Sienna."

"Just my luck," Augustus said with a pained grunt. "He ain't a pushover, either. Hit me like a Space X rocket coming in for a landing on my chest."

"Where are you?" Kat asked, puffing a little.

"Second floor," Augustus said, grunting. "He busted me right through the—AUGHHHHH!"

This time the smashing sound was even more pronounced,

clearer, and I suspected that Augustus had moved up another level inadvertently. "Augustus!" I shouted.

"Yeah," he said, winded. "I'm coming to you. One painful-ass floor at a time …"

"Following," Kat said. "Through the convenient, Augustus-shaped holes in the fl—AHHH!" Something shattered below. "Oops, got seen. Detouring!"

I traded a look with Reed. "We need to—"

"Help them," he said.

"Figure out what they're after," I cut over him, drawing a look of indignation from my soft-hearted brother.

"You're going to leave them to fight this thing on their own?" Reed asked, his eyebrows arching, his body tensing like Dr. Perugini had just tried to transfer that six-foot pole of hers to his ass.

"Yes, I trust them to do their jobs," I said. "A frost giant, however big, is not going to stop Augustus and Kat. And while they're doing that—"

"What the hell is so important here that we're going to abandon our friends—teammates—"

"Son of a—!" Augustus shouted. The unmistakable crash of something going through a floor echoed through the halls behind us as a cloud of dust exploded in one back corner like someone had thrown a sack of flour in the air. When Augustus spoke again, I could hear him clearly, though a little echoey. "Okay. I'm on the fourth floor. Where y'all at?"

A roar followed, echoing through the earpiece and also around the corner behind us. "You go help him," I said, "I'll check out what the iceman—"

"Frost giant," Augustus said.

"On it," Reed said, darting away from me and down the hall, gusting wind and blowing my hair back again.

"I'm like, a floor behind," Kat puffed into my earpiece. "Just hang on."

I ignored her, secure in the knowledge my team had things in hand. A frost giant wasn't that tough, after all, and any surprises that might be waiting behind me … well, Reed, Kat and Augustus were more than a match for them.

I turned my eyes once more to the light streaming into the corridor around the corner, and started forward again, shooting forth at high speed. I needed to know what—if anything—was waiting for me behind that door.

2.

I approached the open door at a hover, feet off the ground. I gave it a quick once-over, wondering what the hell I was looking at. It wasn't a traditionally open and shut door of the sort you'd find on a house. This one was heavier, industrial strength, metal all the way through. There were scorch marks where someone had burned through, leaving black carbonization all around the uneven edges of the hole. It was like what I'd done to the roof, except this was cut through solid steel.

My brain went into a higher alert instantly. Now we had ice on the first floor and evidence of superhot fire or plasma upstairs, which meant that the meta I could hear Reed and Augustus tangling with—I could hear a series of grunts and thumps via the echoing hallway as well as my earpiece—was not the only one in the building.

Gavrikov, I said to myself, and felt the Russian's presence at the forefront of my mind. A Shakespeare quote came to mind from long ago, when my mother had made me memorize long tracts of the Bard: "Fire answers fire, and through their paly flames each battle sees the other's umbered face." Fire was needed to answer fire in my experience, and that experience gave me a bad feeling about what waited ahead.

I listened over the sound of someone—Augustus, I was pretty sure—shouting, "You about to get your ass kicked!" followed by a heavy blow and a grunt of indeterminate origin. A faint gust came around the hallway and blew my

10

hair into my eyes yet again. Damn my brother.

I hoped he was all right.

Faint voices were audible through the burned door, and I listened harder over the battle taking place behind me. This was part of my new resolution not to rush stupidly into places where angels feared to tread. I'd done that a few times in the last handful of years, only to lose more than my fair share of limbs, blood, and consciousness. It was lucky for me that people kept underestimating how much it took to kill me.

"—it's not that simple," an agitated female voice was saying. "I expected—"

"We all expected differently," came a calm, soothing male reply. His voice was like the voice equivalent of butter and jam and honey. Mmm. Hungry. "Can you break through?"

"I don't know," the female voice came back again. She was starting to sound sullen now, as if coming down off her adrenaline high. "I'm wearing out, and I mean, it doesn't even look like—"

"Maybe we should help Gary," another woman's voice broke in, sounding more worried. I tagged the frost giant battling my team Gary. Also, I figured he was old, because no one has named their kid Gary since the seventies.

"You should probably give him a hand," Soothing Voice said. "There are at least four of them out there." I cocked my head as I processed that detail. He knew our numbers? That was an interesting tidbit. My mental alert level ratcheted up another notch since I'd counted three voices now plus the frost giant.

That meant we were evenly matched in the numbers. I didn't like that. Fair fights were bad for your health.

"Are they all fighting Gary?" Worried asked, her voice heavy with concern. Now I wondered if she and Gary were boffing. (She and Gary would boff rather than screw because, again, Gary was old. Follow along, okay?)

Soothing seemed to give that a moment's thought. "No ..." he said finally, concentrating deeply. "Three of them are ..." I heard Kat's screech echo down the hall around me, "... but the fourth ..." There was a moment of silence from the room and then Soothing's voice rose louder, "… is right outside the door, listening to us right now."

"What?" Agitated went right back to her original tone of voice, and I swore I could almost hear her shit a brick. All that was missing was the *clunk!* of it hitting the floor. "I'm gonna—"

"Don't," Soothing said, soothingly, and then he raised his voice again—nicely and politely—and called out, "Come in. I guarantee you safe conduct."

For some reason I couldn't properly explain, I believed him, and went around the corner, ducking my way into the room to a sudden gasp from one of the women waiting in front of me. She had dark, curly hair that twisted its way down in front of eyes the size of tennis balls as she got a load of me. That was Agitated. I could tell by her position in the room and the look she wore that told me she needed a fresh change of undies for that brick she'd shat.

"Welcome," Soothing said, and I took him in with a glance. He was immaculately dressed in a sky-blue dress shirt and khaki trousers. He was a tall fellow, African-American with a deep brown skin tone, and he wore a placid smile. Not a smirk, but a warm, genuine sort of smile. He was standing in front of something that looked like a giant vault in the center of the room. It was contained in the rectangular core of the building, hallways wrapping around it in both directions. It was huge, and it looked like whoever had burned through the door to this room had tried the same trick on the vault door and hadn't met with a similar level of success.

"That's Sienna Nealon," Worried said, swallowing so hard I could almost hear the GULP!

"Fiona," Soothing said, and I tagged her mentally, too. Fiona was Worried.

"We were supposed to be out of here before she showed up," Worried said, and I looked her over as well. She was hanging out a couple steps behind Soothing, and was blond, straight haired, skinny and short enough that she could have ridden a Doberman as her personal steed and looked totally normal doing it. Except the Doberman would have dragged her around thinking she was a bone for him to play with.

"Running from me doesn't typically go so well," I said, probably with less snark than usual. I felt a little muted as I stood there, looking the three of them over.

"We have no quarrel with you," Soothing said.

"Yeah, but the State of Oregon has one with you," I said. "Breaking and entering? I don't know how baked the populace is out here, but I know they still don't take that lightly."

"Oh, funny, a weed joke," Agitated snapped, dark, twirly curls of hair falling over her face. Her eyes went around as something thumped hard against the back wall of the room, out of sight behind the vault. There was a big sign over the vault that said, "WARNING! BIOHAZARD!" along with about fifty of biohazard symbols. It made me wonder just what Palleton Labs was up to out here. "Gary," she muttered, almost under her breath.

"Gary's fine, Amber," Soothing said, giving me a name for Agitated and her twisty black locks. He turned his attention back to me. "We're not looking for any trouble—"

"Most people aren't," I said, "but those that break the law tend to find it landing on the back of their necks anyway." I gave Worried Fiona a glance as she stood up. The carbon scoring along the front of the vault gave me the feeling that she was my Gavrikov, which left only Amber and Soothing as mystery players.

"You say that because you don't know what's happening here," Soothing said, all calm and composed. He even had his hands at his sides, palms facing away from me, probably to give me a sense of being in control. I wasn't under that illusion, but I didn't feel as irritated as I normally did in these circumstances.

"You can feel free to explain it to me once you're in custody," I said. That muted feeling was still heavy in me; I was always one for talking before a fight, but I didn't even feel like fighting. Standing there three-to-one usually would have inspired me to come up with a plan of attack, but here I was, just staring at these three instead of planning my shot order if I had to quickdraw Shadow. "I like a good story as much as the next anger-filled lady." I stared at Fiona and Amber Agitated. "You like stories, right?"

Fiona looked gobsmacked, her skeletal frame looking like bleached bones in a spaghetti-strapped tank top that was barely held up by her thin shoulders. "Yes—no—maybe?" She looked to Soothing for guidance, like I'd thrown her off by calling her out.

"It's a pretty straightforward question," I said, raising an eyebrow.

"And also irrelevant," Soothing said.

"It's sorta relevant," I said, focusing in on him. Something finally broke loose in my head and I realized why I was so damned mellow. "You're an empath, and you're pushing the emotions of the people in this room down."

Soothing's eyebrows rose subtly. "Very good, Sienna. I take it you've dealt with an empath before, then?"

I didn't bite the bait on that one. "I've dealt with all kinds of metas," I said, taking in a long breath as I conjured to mind a strong memory. It didn't take much. "Zack," I whispered.

Yes? Zack Davis responded, answering me in my own head.

"No," Soothing said, his posture changing. He brought up a hand, as though he could stop me. "Don't—"

"I need you to tell me—how did it feel when you died?" I asked him, and the answer came a second later.

A flood of memories burst through my mind, flashes, like repeated slaps to the face, burning at my cheeks. I could see through his eyes, strong hands holding him in place like a parent pushing a squalling baby into an unwanted bath. I could see Clyde Clary holding my hands out, pressing them to his cheeks. There was a searing beneath his skin, an agony that rose as it ripped a scream out of his throat—

"Stop her!" Soothing shouted, his composure lost along with his quiet. He'd gone to full-bore panic as a rush of unfamiliar, uncontrolled emotion dumped into my mind. I wasn't entirely sure how empaths worked, but I doubted he was prepared for the memory of someone dying being poured like boiling water over his icy grip on my feelings.

"No!" Fiona shouted, and she burst into flames from her bony wrists to her skinny shoulders. She drew back a hand and threw it, whipping a solid ball of fire at me.

I brought up a hand and caught it in my palm, snuffing it out with Gavrikov's power. "Feed me rage, guys," I said under my breath.

Oh, this I can do, Eve Kappler said, and I felt a sudden burst of pure anger, loathing so strong I wanted to take the bony specter of Fiona and expose her skeleton to the light of day by peeling her thin skin right off like a blanket. It took me a moment after that to realize that the desire to flay her for raising a hand against me was *probably* not wholly mine. Probably.

I sent three rapid pulses of fire no bigger than a softball back at Fiona and watched her scream and duck out of the way as my fireballs burst against the vault door, showering the area around it with fiery embers. "I thought I was the only Gavrikov left," I muttered. "I thought I was special."

"You're special to us!" Augustus shouted in my earpiece, and I heard a grunt as somebody hit somebody else in the battle outside. "Now kick some ass and come help us with this frost giant!"

I wheeled around to deal with Agitated Amber the curly-haired, but before I could face her, she opened her mouth and screamed at me.

Now I've been known to let a scream or two out in battle, usually to try and intimidate my enemies. Sometimes it works, sometimes it doesn't, and sometimes the results are mixed. I've made people take a few steps back once or twice, made them stop and reconsider, especially when it's the sort of rage-filled scream that warns them that if I get my hands on them, they're going to lose pieces of themselves that they might miss in later life.

This scream, though—it dropped me right to my knees. I don't mean that figuratively, either. My knee hurt as I slammed against the floor, my eyes closed involuntarily, and I felt like I'd been hit by a truck (again). My eyeballs shook in their sockets as though someone had stuck a finger in there, and the pain ran across the front of my body like I was getting one of those Swedish massages of karate chops to my belly, my legs, my boobs, and my face. My teeth vibrated in my jaw, threatening to come loose, and warm liquid seeped out of my ears and down my jawline even as I snotted my upper lip. At least, I thought it was snot at the time. A few seconds later I realized it was blood when I spit out an enormous gob of it, the metallic tang grossing me out.

The sound of Amber's scream was gone after a second or two, but the feeling that it was vibrating my bones persisted. I lowered my head and tried to open my eyes, but my body was shaking like I was still being uncomfortably jarred, constantly. My head was swimming like I'd been dunked in the water and was now floating, lifeless, on the surface. My eyeballs felt like they were dipped in jelly and when I opened them, I could barely see.

Working on healing you, Sienna, Wolfe's gruff voice sounded in my head.

"Work harder," I mumbled. Amber was staring down at me, mouth open, soundless for a second as she took a breath. "Eve?"

Yes?

I threw up a hand as Amber started to speak again and blasted a net of light in a tight ball right in her kisser. It was a precision shot, aimed right for the uvula, and I was surprised I'd made it given that I was so damned dazed from what she'd done to me. The net of light hit the back of her throat and the reaction was instant. She started to gag, and her eyes went from dancing triumph to panic as the net activated her gag reflex.

I rose to my feet and fell on her like a wolf on a lamb. "I bet guys just love sleeping with you, screamer," I said as I punched her lights out with one good shot. All the panic left her as she dropped, unconscious, to the floor of the pre-vault. "Until you melt them to jelly with that voice of yours." I racked my brain for any memory of a meta that could do damage with sound waves. I knew about Sirens, the type that could entangle a mind with pretty words, but this was something different.

I swept my head to the side just in time to catch two

fireballs from Fiona, who was back on her skinny-ass feet. I blasted back with a net of light right to the face and then leapt through the air between us, hammering her skull with one good punch. She thumped back into the vault and slid down, out of the fight.

"Odds are getting better," I mumbled as I cracked my neck to one side. I came around and focused on Soothing, who was against the outer wall, standing there about as peacefully as he could.

"You don't want to do this," he said. "This isn't you."

"Rage and beatings are totally me," I said, advancing on him. "They're pretty much my calling card, actually. Ask anyone who knows me and they'll tell you I'm nothing if not merciless—"

I sensed movement behind me a second before I got creamed. I moved to evade and still caught the punch right behind the ear. It felt as though my stream of conscious thought was a slot machine that just had its lever pulled and came up with an orange, a couple cherries, and brain damage for the last wheel. Because whoever hit me, they knew what they were doing.

I managed to get my head around as I fell, and I caught a perfect still-frame of my attacker's face. I saw it for only a second, even as my mind scrambled to figure out what had just happened. It was a brief glimpse, but enough that I worked it out, that I knew him, and I felt that old familiar feeling start in my belly, a sick sensation that had nothing to do with being cold-cocked from behind.

"Timothy … Logan …" I said from my knees, one elbow keeping me from planting my cheek against the floor.

"I'm sorry, Sienna," he said. He looked like a giant, standing there over me, and I could see the regret in his eyes. He raised his fist nonetheless, though, ready to strike down on me again, and I didn't even have it in me to prepare for the finishing blow.

3.

I was starting to get really used to that sick feeling of betrayal. It was a nasty sensation, rolling in your gut like something you ate that wouldn't give up and move on to torment the next stage of your alimentary canal. I'd felt it quite a few times in my life—James Fries, Erich Winter, Scott Byerly ... they'd all betrayed me in some way or another.

And now Timothy Logan. My first and only parolee from my time as warden for the Cube, the government's metahuman incarceration program.

Hold on, Wolfe apprised me as Logan hesitated a second before striking me down. *Almost got it.*

My thoughts started to clear, but that feeling in my stomach wasn't even close to leaving me. "Why?" I asked as he raised his fist.

"I had no choice," Logan said, and he started to bring his fist down.

"There's always a choice," I said, and mentally I was clear enough to make other plans. *Gavrikov?*

Go.

I blew fire between my lips as Timothy leapt backward. His power was two-second precognition, which meant he knew what I was going to do exactly two seconds before I did it. I knew he'd leap away, but what I really needed to do was get him out of range of knocking the crap out of me right now. That was easy enough; I turned my head and spit a wave of fire in a steady line to either side, guaranteeing he'd have to go backward rather than to either side.

And go backward he did, which left me enough time to leave my knees in a leap sideways and slam my elbow into Soothing's jaw. I wasn't really looking at him, I just elbowed him blind, following the sound of his patient breathing, and was rewarded by a rich cracking sound as I put his damned lights out and landed deftly on my feet. My head was clear and so were my eyes. My heart, though …

Well, that little instrument—its existence much debated on the internet and probably in the minds of the inmates of the Cube—it was clear, too. But it was clear with rage—pure, bonebreaking rage. I turned my eyes on Timothy and I could see his alarm as he realized he was all alone with me, his little friends out of the picture. "Why?" I asked, dripping with malice. "I went to bat for you. I got you out."

"Well," he said, keeping his distance, watching me, probably waiting for his spider sense to warn him when I sprang, "it's not exactly easy getting a job when you've got 'Cube detainee' on your record. These people came to me, they offered money—"

"And you just leapt at the chance to join the brotherhood of criminals again," I said, seething.

"It's not exactly like that, and I think you know it—"

"There's only one thing I know right now," I said, my rage crystallizing into a cool madness. "Hurlyburly."

Timothy frowned, and I could see the wheels spinning in his head. "'Hurlyburly'? What's that?"

"It's my safeword," I said, and shot fire from one hand and nets of light from the other, not really caring which one hit him. He dodged between the two as I kept up the stream and advanced on him, flame penning him in on one quarter and nets of light spattering against the back wall with the other. If the net hit him, he'd be rocketed to the wall and anchored there so I could beat the living shit out of him until this sick feeling of betrayal passed. If the flame hit him, he'd be suffering from disembowelment by inferno. I wasn't picky about which he chose, but I made sure he was going to have to choose one of them.

"Pick your poison," I said, striding toward him as he

retreated, the panic rising on his young face. "Or I'll pick it for you."

"You don't understand, Sienna," he said, visibly sweating as the flames I cast to his side dispersed in a billowing fire against the ceiling. The tiles were burning now, and I didn't care.

"No, you don't understand," I said. "I'm the line, and you've crossed me." I opened my mouth again and blasted him with a net of light shot right from my gaping maw. I'd never done that before. I'd been tempted to go with the fire instead, but somehow the light won out.

Timothy, with nowhere to dodge, caught the net in the center of his chest. Strands burst free and wrapped around him, hauling him back as I killed the bursts of flame. He slammed into the blackened wall as I drew the last of the fire out of the ceiling, snuffing it. Smoke hung thick in the air and a fire alarm rang in the distance. I fired four more nets and bound Timothy's arms and legs tightly to the wall, which I realized was also metal.

The sprinkler system kicked on, spraying down on me with vile-smelling water, my hair dripping down my face in seconds. I kept coming at him, and he watched me, trussed up to the wall like a pig ready for roasting. I was a foot away when I threw my first punch. I put all that hurt, all that betrayal—those of a lifetime—into that punch.

Which is to say I pulled it, because I didn't want him to die right away.

His head rocked back and hit the steel wall, and he blinked hard. I could almost see little birdies flying in there as he tried to focus himself. "Uh …" he said, opening his mouth. Blood dripped out, washed free by saliva and the sprinklers. "… Hurlyburly?"

I stared at him evenly. "That's *my* safeword." I got up in his face so I could look him clear in the eye, my nostrils flaring like I was Wolfe on a kill, smelling his fear. "There's nowhere safe for you, Timothy." And I jacked him in the jaw once again, and again after that, but stopped when his head lolled to mark his passage into unconsciousness. Apparently there was somewhere safe for him, after all.

4.

By the time I checked on Reed, Augustus and Kat, they had almost subdued the frost giant. I rolled my eyes hard at them, Augustus with a big block of dirt as a choker against the dude's neck, Reed trying to pull the oxygen out of his lungs enough to knock him out, and Kat—tiny Kat—riding the frost giant's shoulders and punching him pitifully in the head.

I rocked him out with one punch and he crumbled, his ice armor shattering into a billion tiny shards.

"Nice of you to remember the little people," Reed said, massaging a black and blue contusion around his neck.

"That looks painful," I said, and knelt to scoop up some of Frosty's shield detritus, which I promptly tossed to Reed, who caught it. "You should put some ice on that."

"Hilarious," Reed pronounced. "What did you find in the—"

"Four metas," I said. "All down."

"Man, we couldn't even take out their sentry," Augustus said, eyeing the unconscious body of the frost giant. "Are you sure you need a team?"

"Teamwork makes the dream work," I muttered. I couldn't remember who I was quoting. It was an empty platitude, and I could see by the looks on their faces that they weren't any more reassured by it than I was. "We're going to need meta containment pods. We have a Gavrikov, an empath, a short-duration pre-cog, and a ... I dunno, a screamer, I guess, not sure what to call her."

21

"A screamer?" Kat looked up from where she was bent double, hands on her knees. "What's that supposed to mean?"

"She screams, and I think sound waves come out."

"That's generally what happens when one screams," Reed said.

"Yeah, well," I rolled my eyes, "her screams turn human tissue into jelly. Probably can break glass and bust walls, too."

"Ohhhhh," Augustus said, nodding at last. "Man. I was wondering how you knew she was a screamer. I mean, my mind can't be the only one that went right into the gutter—"

"It was," I said.

"No," Reed said, looking marginally guilty. "It wasn't."

"I still have no idea what you guys are talking about," Kat said, finally returning to standing, parking her hands on her hips.

"We need to tag and bag these rejects," I said, nodding at Frosty the Giant-man. I hadn't heard any of them in my ear since Screamin' Amber burst my eardrums, and I ran a hand down the side of my face. It came back bloody, and I realized she must have literally burst my eardrums, because there was a trail up to my ear canals, and my earpiece was missing. "Someone patch the cops in and have them bring in our restraints. Also, a chem kit so we can dose them."

"I'll do it," Augustus said, heading back down the hall and giving Frosty a solid kick as he did so. He fiddled with his earpiece and then started to speak. "Portland PD, this is task force Signet—"

"Who the hell chose that lame name?" Reed asked.

"I did," Kat said, sounding irritated. "You wanted to me to interface with the Portland PD while you prepped—"

"—the building is clear," Augustus said, "no remaining hostiles on their feet. We need our chem kit and restraints, please."

"He's so polite," I said, staring after him. "I'd be barking orders."

"Did you ... have a fight?" Reed asked, sidling close to me in the hallway.

I gave him a hard look as I meandered over to Frosty and grabbed him by the sleeve, taking particular care not to touch his skin. "Why, yes. Yes, I did. While you three were dicking around with Frosty the Snowdouche, I was beating the ass off four other metas, including Timothy Logan —" Reed cringed, "—who is just so lucky he's not a corpse right now."

"Who is Timothy Logan?" Kat asked.

"Ouch," Reed said. "But I wasn't talking about that kind of fight. I meant with your ..." He lowered his voice, like Kat couldn't hear him anyway, "... gentleman caller?"

"What is this, a Jane Austen novel?" I dragged Frosty along as Reed followed and Kat subtly did the same, a dozen steps behind him, plainly eavesdropping. "If you're talking about Jeremy, he's my boyfriend, and no, we didn't have a fight. Have you lost your sense and sensibility?"

"You just seem a little off," Reed said.

"He means that you are super, super bitchy today," Kat said, oh-so-helpfully. "Like someone lit the fuse on your tampon."

I hurled Frosty bodily into the room with the others and heard a satisfying *SMACK!* as he hit the vault wall and slid down. (He was a meta, you sensitive souls, he was fine.) "No one lit a fuse on my anything. If I'm cantankerous, maybe it's because I'm sick and tired of trying to keep assholes like this in line and seeing not one ounce of rehabilitation happening." I threw a glance over my shoulder at Timothy and stuffed back a wad of resentment that threatened to surge out.

"What?" Reed looked genuinely concerned, leaning forward on the balls of his feet like that might help him catch whatever I came out with next.

"Never mind, it doesn't matter." I stormed into the center room through the burned-out door and gave each of the perps a good, solid, painful kick to make sure they were all still out. There wasn't a twitch to any of their faces, which told me they were either safely unconscious or they were masters at controlling their pain. I doubted it was the latter, because *I'd* already racked every single one of them up and knew that they made faces when they hurt.

"It matters a little," Kat said, easing into the room behind Reed, "if only because we're hoping that if you get it all out ... maybe we can hug, and you'll go back to being kinda-happy Sienna again. Which is nice. It's been really pleasant these last few months. You've almost been like a different person. But today ..." She looked at my handiwork with the criminals laid out around us. "It's like you've taken a step back to ... I dunno, just-post-Directorate-raging-bull-Sienna?"

I gave her an evil look, because I remembered damned well her betrayal of the Directorate, though I had (mostly) let it go a long while back. "How long have we been doing this?"

Reed looked taken aback. "Uhhh ... uhm ... I mean, I know it feels like forever sometimes ..."

"Six years," said Kat promptly. "Almost seven."

"Does it feel like it's getting any better?" I asked. "Do you ever get the sense that we're making a difference? That maybe out there somewhere, some meta's making a decision not to be a heinous shithole and criminal just because we're beating the asses of those who do and taking away their freedom? I mean, look at this crew." I threw my hands wide to encompass this group that we'd knocked out—that'd I'd knocked out. "They did this, risking waking up in the Cube every day for the rest of their lives. Because they've made their choices, and we can't trust them in society anymore."

"Uhh," Reed said, sounding like he was picking his words carefully, "this sounds like the sort of debate you don't usually want to have ..." I suspected he was looking for the landmine that would inevitably blow his leg off.

"What's the purpose, Reed?" I asked. "Stop them and drop them in a prison where they can't ever re-offend? Protect those outside by sealing these morons forever in stasis? Does it stop any of the other idiots who are yet to come? Or does it just keep these knuckleheads from causing any more trouble?" I hung my head. "I mean ... we don't even deal with the human threats out there, really, and normal humans can do more than a fair amount of damage without powers." I felt like a ten-billion-ton weight had settled on my shoulders. "What the hell is the point? Are we even making a difference?"

Reed looked pained, but his argument came fast. "I dunno, why don't you ask the families of the people Thunder Hayes killed if you've made a difference. Or the survivors of Crow Vincent, or Yvette Mulcahy, or—"

"I know their names," I said softly. "I know … all their names."

"You've never been quite like this before," Kat said, her face all screwed up in concentration. "Say … is this about that Supreme Court decision that's supposed to come out today—?"

Reed closed his eyes, then opened them, then rolled them all in sequence. "Subtle, Kat. Way to draw the obvious line."

I stood there silent for a long moment. "Yes."

"Oh. Well. Okay, then," Kat said. She bobbed uselessly in the doorway for a moment then nodded once. "I'm gonna go see how Augustus is coming along with those restraints and the chem kit. I'll, uh … be back." She ducked out the door and disappeared into the hall in a flash of blond hair.

"What if … it's all been for nothing, Reed?" I asked. My brother stood there like a great statue, unmoving. "My entire life's work, undone with one judgment."

"It's not for nothing," he said, and now he sounded like the empath with the soothing voice. "You saved the world, Sienna. No matter what else comes out today … they can't take that away from you."

I heard his words, but it was like my eardrums were still ruptured, because they fell deafly upon them. We stood in silence, waiting for the restraints and the means to contain these criminals that I'd beaten. They were just a few more of a seemingly infinite number I'd removed from society, from doing harm to others, and I wondered if any of it, any of it at all, had ever even mattered.

5.

"It is grim up in here," Augustus pronounced once we were all loaded on the private jet chartered for us by our new employer and up in the air. Portland PD had released the prisoners to us so we could transport them to the Cube, and we'd gotten grudging permission from the federal authorities to act as the ferryboat for these clowns. It was on the way for us anyhow, and I had no problem staring at these mooks for a few hours while we flew back to Minneapolis. They were all sleeping, anyway, save for Timothy Logan, who I'd trussed up properly in a stabilized metal frame that was a little like a chair with arm restraints. He couldn't move anything but his mouth and he was wisely keeping that still presently, though his eyes were darting around, taking in everything going on in the plane's cabin as we cruised at thirty thousand feet. "What did I miss?" Augustus asked.

"Sienna is experiencing a mid-life crisis centered around a dearth of purpose," Kat said. "Honestly, this would be such a great storyline if you'd just let my producers film—"

"No," I said.

"Is this about that SCOTUS thing?" Augustus asked, brow all furrowed.

"Ew, gross," Kat said, sticking her tongue out in disgust. "Why are we talking about some guy's SCOTUS? It's like, the least attractive part of any human body, ever."

Reed just stared at her. "SCOTUS stands for Supreme Court of the United States."

"Ah *ha*!" Augustus said, pointing a finger at Kat. "Now

whose mind is in the gutter?"

"Look, Sienna," Reed said, leaning over to me. The plane was laid out so that all the chairs were facing the middle; Reed and I were turned around to look back at Logan and the prisoners, while Kat and Augustus were sitting among them nearer the rear of the cabin. "I know this feels like a slap in the face of everything you've done, but we don't know how it's going to turn out yet. They could make a narrow ruling that upholds indefinite detention for meta criminals, or a broad one that allows for even more expansive powers—"

"Or they could slap it down," I said, "and turn loose everyone we've ever incarcerated." Which was what the TV pundits had been predicting based on the hearing. I had avoided the hearing coverage at the time, but as we crept closer and closer to the release of rulings, I had an increasingly bad feeling about what was coming.

"Even if they do," Reed said, with the patient air of a professor lecturing a first-year law student, "no one's saying we can't jail these people." He indicated our new prisoners with a wave of the hand. "But there should be trials and due process, not just arbitrary, infinite sentences."

"Yeah, I mean," Augustus said, "it's always kind of bothered me that we're sending these people away for life without parole. Don't get me wrong, we've dealt with some bad people, but … they aren't all murderers. These folks didn't kill anyone, for instance." He looked warily at Frosty, who was head and shoulders above the rest of Logan's lot. "Though not for lack of trying, in some cases."

"Let's say they overrule indefinite detention," Reed said, "maybe that's a good thing. Maybe it'll finally force Congress to deal with the meta problem."

"Because Congress is exceptional at solving problems without creating even bigger ones in the process," I snarked.

Reed sighed lightly. "You know that's the sarcastic, offhand response."

"Yet also the true one."

"These people are our elected officials," Reed said with an air of great patience, "and whether we are totally happy with them or not, they're the legislature and this is their responsibility. They should pass a law making the use of metahuman powers in the commission of a crime a federal offense and a felony. Boom. That takes the burden of incarcerating people who can't easily be imprisoned off the states and local jurisdictions, and adds a little extra oomph for prosecuting a meta who's used their abilities to commit a crime."

"Gah, Reed," I said, putting my hand in my face, "I am fully aware of the flaws of the current system but I caught almost all these people red-handed in the commission of felonies." I went on, undeterred. "Pretty much all of them resisted arrest violently—"

"That's true, they don't seem to come quietly along, do they?" Kat mused.

"To forever jail? Gee, I wonder why," Augustus said.

"—and so I'm sorry, but I don't feel the need shed big fat crocodile tears over locking them up into infinity," I finished, sitting back in my seat and crossing my arms. "These aren't ambiguous cases, most of them. Metas aren't shy about what they do—like that jag in San Fran. Think about the loot he had spread out over his shithole place. He wasn't even hiding his ill-gotten gains."

"That was some bling," Augustus said. "Did we take that into evidence? Because I'm thinking we've got enough that if one or two diamonds disappeared, ain't nobody gonna—"

"The SFPD took it into evidence," Reed said.

"Clearly Augustus isn't worried about lawful consequences," I said. "Kinda illustrating my point."

"This isn't about contrition, or how guilty they are. Even in our new extra-governmental capacity, our job should be to catch these guys and help make the case against them. If they try and kill you, hey, tell the court about it. That should be our role, like in traditional law enforcement—help make the case for why these people should be off the streets. But it's not our job to determine their punishment or the duration. We get to see the crime up close, and sometimes that doesn't leave us with a clear head about who they are or what they deserve." He looked significantly at Timothy Logan. "That's supposed to be for a jury of their peers to decide, or an impartial judge."

"Let me know when you find a totally impartial judge," I said, looking out the window. The sun was up outside the airplane, shining brightly in a clear sky. "I have a feeling you'll be looking for a while, because everybody has feelings about these things. No one's a philosophical blank, Reed. Some judges believe in the iron hammer of deterrence and some seem to think repeat-offender dickheads like Logan here just need a little belly rub to make them sweet, productive members of society."

"How do you know what it takes to make someone a productive member of society?" Reed asked. He sounded sincere, if a little wary.

"I don't," I said, "but the recidivism rate seems to be near a hundred percent based on my experience—"

"You let one guy out," Kat said. "I'm no scientist—"

"Obvs," I snapped.

"—but that's an awfully small sample."

"So we should just go with the 'lock 'em up forever' strategy?" Augustus asked. "One strike and you're out?"

"These weren't mistakes," I said, glaring at Timothy Logan, who wisely continued to stay silent. "These were choices."

"Because you've never made a bad choice?" Reed asked quietly.

"Plenty of them," I said, "but I also worked my way out of them. Like purgatory, or indentured servitude."

"Whoa," Augustus said, "you think the scales are balanced for killing people because you did government service?"

"I killed killers," I said coldly.

"Was Rick Gerasimos a killer?" Kat asked, sounding genuinely perplexed.

"He was the head of the preeminent meta criminal organization in the world," I said. "Unless you believe Omega just changed direction suddenly under his leadership." I was hot and defensive about it, for probably obvious reasons of self-justification. "So, yes, in most courts of law, if you could prove Omega was a criminal enterprise linked to murder, he could have been tried for it."

"You didn't try him for it, though, you beat him to death with a chair," Reed said. "Murder is murder, Sienna. And if we become the tribunal, the judge and jury for these people … look, our system is imperfect, you get no argument from me. But to bastardize the words of Churchill, it's the worst system except for all the others. If we impose vengeance on people, just hammer them down, jail them forever, make no attempt to reconcile them with society … how does that make us any better, any different, than them?"

"Because we don't prey on the innocent," I snapped back. "And if you can't see that difference, you're blind."

"Like justice?" Reed asked.

"Was Palleton Labs innocent?" Timothy Logan spoke up at last, apparently casting off that vestige of good sense I thought he still had. "Do you have any idea what they were doing there?"

"Do you?" I asked, glaring him down. "Because it sounded to me like you took a job just because you needed the money, not because you believed in some righteous cause of robbing from some biotech company to give plague vaccines to the poor or something."

His gaze flicked away, and I could see I'd struck him right in the guilty conscience. Part of me wanted to know if he was holding something back about the lab; that vault had remained sealed, and I hadn't met the owners of the company before I'd left Portland. I didn't like mysteries, as a rule, but I had no time to worry about it now. Besides, I hadn't been hired to dig on this one.

"Innocence and guilt is a blurry line, Sienna," Reed said. I was running right to the edge of my patience with his calm, lecturing demeanor. "It moves depending on which side of it you're on—"

"It doesn't matter," I cut him right off. "Because it's out of my hands, out of your hands." I settled back in my seat. "Now it's in the hands of nine unelected, unaccountable people—philosopher kings and queens, if you will. Their judgment gets to win out." I smiled at him, but it was a nasty one, befitting the dark mood I was in.

Silence fell for a few minutes, then stretched into an hour, then two. Reed stared out the window, his tanned face lit by the glowing sun. Augustus kept his eyes anchored on the prisoners, doing his duty. I did the same, though less diligently. Kat had put her headphones in her ears at some point and was jamming out to Meghan Trainor. I couldn't fault her for that.

"We're beginning our initial descent into Minneapolis," the pilot broke in to announce a little while later. I could see the lone steward lingering near the front of the galley, just listening to us. He'd offered us drinks when the flight started, but he'd withdrawn when the argument began. I had a feeling he was being very smart and strategic about this. I wouldn't have wanted to walk into the line of fire or the cold freeze between the four of us at the moment, either, if I were human. "The seatbelt sign is on."

"I always forget to go to the bathroom until it's too late," Augustus said as the ding of the seatbelt warning echoed through the cabin.

"It's a private plane," Reed said, stirring out of his solemn silence, "and you're a meta. You can survive a crash landing from the bathroom, Augustus. Just go."

Augustus bolted for the rear head, zipping up the aisle without hesitation, his seatbelt clanking as he jetted to the lavatory. I watched the prisoners carefully, taking up his job while he was gone. Kat bopped her head to her tune.

"It's going to be okay, you know," Reed said under his breath. I looked sideways at him, and found him speaking to me from beneath a hand that covered his mouth, hiding his reassurance from Kat. "Whatever the ruling, we'll keep going. We'll keep making a difference."

I blinked and then glanced at Timothy Logan, who quickly averted his eyes when he realized I was looking at him. Gutless, he couldn't even look at me. "We'll see," I said, as Augustus swept up the aisle and back to his seat.

We landed a few minutes later, and taxied for a few minutes after that. Reed had his phone out, the glare off the screen blinding me for a moment before he put it down. I could tell by the look on his face that something was wrong.

"What?"

He tried to force a smile, but failed. "They ruled."

Ice raced through my veins. "And?" The plane lurched to a stop, along with my stomach.

Reed stared at me for an interminably long moment, and then the door of the plane opened. Light spilled in from outside, along with a chilly breath of autumn wind. "They overturned indefinite detention. And …"

"And what?" Augustus threw in. He was hanging off the edge of his seat, his belt already undone.

"It's complicated, but … they're not allowing new trials of existing prisoners. They're basically letting them off for whatever with time served." He grimaced. "I don't fully understand it, but if a prosecutor wants to go after them … I think they're going to have to do so for a new crime."

"All the all the outs in free," I said under my breath.

"Does this mean I can leave?" Timothy Logan said, and I heard Kat gasp.

"Bad timing," Kat said when she composed herself a second later. I didn't even realize she'd been listening.

I undid my seatbelt and stood, leering down at Timothy. I could feel the betrayal, the anger, the hatred for who and what he represented. It was eating at me, gnawing at my stomach like a bad meal. I wanted him to pay for what he'd done, but more than that, I wanted him to pay for his crime against me.

"I …" Logan said, pale as cream. "Sienna, I didn't … please don't …"

"Sienna," Reed said softly, "he's not worth it."

"You're right," I choked out, still anchored to my place in the cabin. I could smell fresh air beyond the door, calling to me, and I didn't wait. I blew past the steward and shot out the door, keeping low over the Eden Prairie airport until I was clear of their airspace, and then I took to the skies, knowing that almost everything I'd done in my life up to this point was all for naught.

6.

"Come in."

I did as the voice bade, pushing carefully through the wooden door with its placard marked "Dr. Quinton Zollers," and taking care not to loose my rage on an inanimate object, especially one belonging to a friend. More than a friend, really. Dr. Zollers had been with me from nearly the beginning, after all.

"You knew I was coming?" I asked as I closed the door behind me. It felt like I was barely holding it all back, like I could explode at any moment. That was a real danger for someone with the living bomb of a Gavrikov trapped beneath her skin, too.

"Even if I didn't have a close bond with you, it'd be hard for a telepath to miss that cloud of rage streaking across the Minneapolis skyline like a comet ready to put an end to some dinosaurs," Zollers said with his typical dry humor.

"I could think of about nine I'd like to make extinct this morning," I fumed.

"Five," Zollers corrected. When I looked at him quizzically, he said, "They didn't all rule against it, after all. The court was divided."

"Did you read the decision?" I asked. I hadn't, so I was morbidly curious if anyone had added a few stinging, sniping condemnations of my actions as proxy for the government.

"I skimmed it while I was waiting for you," Zollers said, holding up his phone before he tossed it carefully onto the table to his right. He was always so gentle, even with meta strength. "They kept to the substance of the arguments."

I flopped down on the couch where I usually spent our sessions. "You knew I was worried what they'd say about me."

"For someone who takes a punch like a champ," Zollers said, interlacing his fingers in front of his face and leaning back in his chair, utterly relaxed despite being stuck in a room with the most dangerous human being on the planet, "you do tend to be easily nettled by the opinions of others."

"Weird, isn't it?" I stared up at the ceiling, which was all smoothed-out, fog-textured rather than the stupid nasty popcorn stuff. "I'm a walking contradiction."

"You're a wounded person," he said. "That's different."

"After all this time, I'm still wounded?" I pouted. "And here I thought I was finally well-adjusted."

"The scars of a childhood filled with psychological and physical abuse and isolation don't just fade away under meta healing power, Sienna." He sounded as serious as I'd ever heard him. "You can take a punch, get shot, have your arms and legs burned and blown off … but what your mother did to you lingers." His voice was low, but slightly rougher today than usual, and it took me a minute to realize that he was modulating his tone to avoid the register Soothing Voice had used when trying to talk me out of beating the shit out of his merry band. "You viewed her as the source of all authority, and so when other kinds of authority come to bear on you—peer groups, the media, government—you don't tend to take it well."

"My mommy issues extend to my relationship with the government?" I snorted, still staring at the ceiling.

"And father issues, too."

"Naturally. Because it couldn't be simple."

"Criticism seldom is," he said. "And this criticism … it's not even a criticism. It's the force of law—"

"Emphasis on 'force.'"

He stopped to compose his thoughts then went on, now in his regular voice, like he didn't care anymore if it tripped my trigger. "We get to decide as a society—in a somewhat roundabout way, via our elected officials and who they appoint to these positions of power—what kind of rules we want to live under. This is the exercise of that mechanism. You can't view it as a personal repudiation. It's settling a point of law that hasn't been dealt with in any society in history." I lifted my head to see him smiling. "Not since the days before the gods went underground has any system of government been forced to truly address the inequalities of force present between humans and metas. The ancient societies dealt with it in one way—the gods could do whatever the hell they wanted. We went the opposite direction at first, reacted perhaps too strongly, calling for a harsh response to the use of meta powers on humans." He steepled his fingers in front of him. "Now we're striking the balance and saying that metas are subject to the same laws as humans, with the same burdens of proof and the same standards applied to everyone else."

"Metas can do more damage in shorter order than humans," I said, leaning back into the soft couch, feeling the effects of a night of missed sleep. "They can evade better than human criminals, leave less sign … they're not even in the same league."

"We're not gods, Sienna."

"We used to be," I said, almost in a whisper. "We're still god-like, and even though humans can kill us now, they can't always do it fast enough." I took a deep breath. "I ran into a Gavrikov tonight. I didn't think there were any left, but we ran across another one. That's two in the last year."

"And that worries you because a Gavrikov can—"

"It worries me because no matter what sort of arguing anyone does about weapons in the hands of civilians, no one is carrying a nuke around," I said. "But a Gavrikov *is* a nuke. An infinite, never-ending nuclear bomb that they could deploy over and over again, until every city in the world was just ash in the damned wind." I folded my arms over myself. "Or how about one of those metas that produces deadly bio-toxins? Refine it a little, put it in a bomb, set it to the prevailing winds, and pffffft—a million people die choking to death on their own blood. I've even heard of metas that can produce deadly diseases … basically every type of WMD is covered in the spectrum of meta ability, and we are left without any recourse to stop these people before they do something terrible."

"You have the law," he said.

"I'm sure the law will be a sweet consolation when New York City is a smoking ruin, or LA is a permanently quarantined biohazard zone, or Washington, DC, is a disease-infested wasteland." I pursed my lips and frowned. "I guess that last thing has sort of already happened. But my point is that a meta doesn't have the barrier to entry that's required of a human to pull off an honest-to-gosh WMD attack. No plutonium, no anthrax, no mustard gas. They just show up and wreak havoc."

"You're worried because you're afraid you can't stop it." His voice was soft, and I turned my head to look at him. "If any of those things rear their head ... you're worried you won't be able to stop it in time."

"If *they* even want me to," I said, sullen with self-pity. "You can say all day that this decision isn't a repudiation of me, but who else has been putting away meta criminals? I've been gone from the Agency for months, and I'm still hauling in bad guys. I don't even think Scott and Guy Friday are working, they're just jerking off somewhere in a government office in DC—"

"Which explains the disease-infested wasteland."

"Careful." I frowned at him. "I did date one of those knuckleheads, after all."

"Then clearly the disease came from the other one."

"Probably," I conceded with a faint smile. "Friday probably wears that mask for a reason, after all." I went quiet for a bit, and he let me sit in silence. "Yes, I worry about what will happen. But even more than that ... I wonder what the point was?" I turned my head to see him watching me, concerned as always. "Reed says we did good, that we kept some bad guys from doing bad things, or continuing to do bad things, but part of me wonders ... is this it? Is this all there is? Because I don't know that even before this ruling if I was doing one iota of real good." I settled my head back on the couch.

"It's a common lament among humans and metahumans alike, you know," Zollers said. "That feeling where you wonder if you're doing anything worthwhile with your life. It takes flight in the form of passion in youth, worry in middle age, and regret among the old. You're hardly the first person to feel it, but you might just be the only who can claim to have actually saved the world and still be wondering if your life counts for anything."

"Maybe I just wonder … if this is all there is?" The soft couch beneath my head threatened to lull me to sleep, or swallow me up in its comfortable cushions. "Kill bad guys, stop bad guys … occasionally date a guy … maybe get laid … eat some imported Terry's Chocolate Oranges while Netflixing *Sherlock* … is that all there is?"

"There's also *Luther*."

"Smartass."

"Dogs don't wonder why they exist, Sienna," he said. "Humans are unique in that regard, full of questions about their purpose. I can't answer it for you, either, because everyone has to come to their own answer. It's Philosophy 101, and anyone who says they have a universal truth for you to answer your question … well, you might want to treat them with a little skepticism."

"I just don't want to waste my life working for nothing," I said. I felt the regret part of it, like at the ripe age of twenty-four I qualified for the last stage of existential angst. "You can talk all day about how I saved the world, but that was years ago, and what I've done since … well, that sandcastle just got knocked over by the tide."

"It's up to you whether to decide to build it again, I guess," he said, serious once more. "People build sandcastles every day—and homes, and lives and all manner of things. And they don't build them because they're going to last forever. Nothing does. Some day, our sun will burn out, our planet will die, and long before even that happens everything we are and have done will have been forgotten. As long as you might live, you won't be anything but dust by the time the earth comes to its natural end … but people build anyway. They do it for the day, because we're here now, and because in this moment it shows that these are the things that matter to us. That are important to us. Beauty doesn't last, and neither does life … and neither does your work." He leaned forward, and I saw him smile. "But just because a thing doesn't last forever doesn't mean we shouldn't do it. This quest to protect people … you don't do it because it'll 'echo in eternity'— to steal a phrase from Russell Crowe in *Gladiator.*"

"It's a good thing you told me where it came from, because you had me all ready to slaughter some Germanic hordes."

His smile grew wider, and I felt reassured as he delivered the cherry on top to his speech, a warm reassurance in a world that had felt suddenly cold. "You do it because protecting people is important to you." He grew quiet for a long minute, and when he spoke, he sounded serious. "You do it … because it's who you are, Sienna."

7.

A couple hours later, I had transferred from Dr. Zollers's couch to my own. My attention drifting, I half absorbed the constant analysis being fed to me by the cable news channel on my TV. The reporter on screen at the moment was framed by wooded land in the background, and the chyron of streaming words at the bottom proclaimed, "METAHUMAN DETAINEES RELEASED FROM MINNESOTA PRISON." It said other things, too, and so did the reporter, but I barely noticed them as I lifted a margarita glass to my lips and took a long sip of salty goodness after first raising a toast to the moron jabbering on the screen. "Here's to you, decision makers," I said. "I hope you're wiser than I am. Cuz releasing all the meta criminals sounds like a stupid idea to me, but I guess I'm kinda drunk."

There was a click of a key in the door, and I turned my head in time to see it open and Ariadne appear in shadow, her red hair highlighted by the fading rays of the sun. "Oh, thank God you're here," she said, letting out a sigh of very obvious relief as she shut it behind her.

"Where else would I be?" I wondered as I sipped my margarita. It was homemade, from a mix and a lot of tequila. "Work seems kinda pointless at the moment."

"Well, that's where I was," she said with some annoyance. "I just—I heard this morning, and when the rest of the gang came back without you ... well, I worried how'd you'd react to all this."

"Did you try calling?"

"About fifty times, yeah."

"Hmmm," I said, swirling the ice in the bottom of my wide-mouthed glass. "What did I do with my phone?" I shifted in my seat and sent a probing hand down the back of my pants. I fished it out of my pocket and pulled it up to reveal the screen lit with about twenty missed calls. "According to this, you overstated it by thirty."

"Well, it was a lot," Ariadne said, peering over my shoulder at the phone.

"Why were you worried how I would react to all this?" I asked, tossing my phone on the table beside me. "Clearly I'm fine."

"Because drinking a margarita big enough to fill a toilet bowl is 'fine'?"

"I also went to see Dr. Zollers," I said, raising my glass to hide my mouth. "Whatever, I don't question your coping mechanisms." I paused as something occurred to me. "And, hey, these are *your* margarita glasses!"

"I'm not questioning anything," she said. "I'm just worried. I don't want to see you do anything rash."

"I'm not going to do much of anything at all, thanks," I said, tipping back my glass. "I'm just gonna sit here, finish my drink, maybe have another, and wait for the world to explode so I can say, 'Haha, no thanks, for real just help yourselves.'"

She sagged a little. "You're not … really going to do that, are you?"

"Probably not," I admitted. "But sometimes it's fun to imagine you're more important than you are. It's a good salve for wounded pride, you know." I sipped my margarita. "And so is this."

Ariadne made her way around me toward the kitchen where she dropped her bag, then hung up her keys on the ring over the counter. Light from the rear windows of the house illuminated her fiery red hair here as well, and she looked stern. "You know what else is good for that?" she asked. "Sensible action."

"We don't do that sort of shit around here, thank you very

much." I snorted. "Sensible action. Puh-lease. That's a contradiction in terms to this girl—"

I was going to say more, drunkenly expound upon the idea of my role in society as both arbiter of justice and also occasional dragon of furious vengeance, but I didn't get a chance to finish waxing rhapsodic because a long shadow stretched through my living room window and then the wall exploded inward.

I held tight to my margarita glass as the window shards dusted my face and pieces of wood and drywall plaster plumed into the air in a cloud of dust.

"Hellooooo," came a drawling, country-fried voice that was filled with raw anger and dumb amusement all in one. A hulking shadow swayed into my living room, followed by another. Sunlight glinted off the steel skins of the two morons who'd just had the raw nerve to invade my living room. A couple more feminine figures followed behind, one of them coughing and hacking at the dust in the air. "Anybody home?" came the bullhorn voice again.

"And you were worried how *I'd* react?" I tossed back at Ariadne, thankfully far from the front of the house, her eyes and the top of her head barely visible where she was ducking behind the kitchen counter. I settled my gaze on the intruders who'd just burst through the front of my home, and the surviving members of the Clary family—newly freed from the Cube—locked their ratlike eyes on me through the dust.

"We got a bone to pick with you, Sienna Nealon," one of them—I think it was Clyde, Jr., but it could have been Buck. I couldn't keep track of them, especially with their skin all covered up in steel coating.

"You want to fight me again, you miserable little skidmarks?" I tossed back the last of my margarita in one gulp before tossing aside the glass. It shattered against the wall (because why not?), and I floated upright out of the chair, secretly happy for an outlet with which to vent all the frustrations of the day. "Let's rumble, you shitstains."

8.

Alcohol plus the events of the day conspired to make me angry enough to drop kick a Clary or four, and lucky me, here they were. Like a pizza with all the right toppings showing up to your door when you're hungry, but you didn't order it. (That happened to me once.) Four Clarys, two fists, no waiting.

The two big guys bum rushed me, because of course they would. They thought with their tiny metal dongs and not anything inside their skulls. Ma Clary had been the brains of that family; the rest were a bunch of bottom-of-the-barrel yokels for whom I spared all the consideration I might for a pile of dog crap. I don't care where it comes from, what it looks like, but if it gets on the bottom of my shoe, I will go ape shit.

I rocketed at high speed against the first of them, slowing and darting between his legs. He tried to track and follow me, but he was a little too slow, in terms of both coordination and cognitive process. I grabbed his ankles and gave a solid, Wolfe-powered yank. His face met the carpet, and then I grabbed his legs and suplexed him into the girl standing behind him. Her bones crunched against his steel skin, and whatever her power or name might have been, it no longer mattered, cuz she was out of the fight and hopefully dead.

What? It was technically self-defense, and in spite of whatever bravado I might have projected to these four numbskulls, the last thing I needed right now was her to rise again and stab me to death while I was tangling with the other three.

"You li'l bitch!" the other Clary female screamed as I came back up after my suplex. Her hair snaked forward, a living thing. Ugh, I hated Medusa types. Her hair wrapped around me, snug and tight around my arms, rising up to my neck like a noose.

Did I say, "like a noose"?

I lit off the Gavrikov power and she screamed as I burned my way through her snakey locks. I reached up and grabbed her hair just north of where I burned it, dragging her toward me. I directed the fire out of my hands and up her hair, and watched it climb up her locks. She screamed and danced, somewhat trapped by the way I was holding her hair as the flames crawled toward her head. I kept up the fire and she tore free and fell into the bushes, screaming and rolling as she tried to stop the flames from burning her scalp. I bet it was going to leave her with a dandruff problem regardless.

"What the helllll—" the last of the Clarys left standing was another of those stoneskin mooks, and he apparently had some deathly slow reflexes, because he'd just stood there and stared as I ran through three of his relatives like White Castle mixed with Ex-Lax. I didn't waste a second waiting for his ineptitude to vanish. I lunged forward with two fingers extended and gave him the ol' Three Stooges right to the eyes, sinking them in up to the knuckles. "AAAAAAAGHHHHHHHHHH!" he screamed.

I could have killed him with a simple release of firepower, but I decided—or maybe the alcohol did—to be merciful. I turned and used my super strength to pick him up by the eye sockets, ignoring his mewling cries, and rammed him and his metal head right into his brother/cousin/lover/all of the above. The resulting sound was like ringing a gong. It echoed through the neighborhood and sounded a little like the noise Screamin' Amber had produced back in Portland before I shut her mouth.

"Unghhh," one of the male Clarys moaned as the sound of their stupid skulls clanging together died down. For good measure, I banged them together again, and it produced another rich, resonant tone. It sounded kinda good, like maybe the start of a classic metal song, so I did it about eight more times, until they stopped moaning.

"Okay, I think they're unconscious, you can stop now!" Ariadne shouted from the kitchen. I looked back. She was standing there with a pained look on her face, fingers jammed deep in her ears.

I clanged them together once more for good measure to bring my new composition to a close, and as I finished their skin lost its metallic luster, shifting back to flesh. "Now I'm done, I think." But I smacked them together again. What? It wasn't like they had brains to damage.

"What about that one?" Ariadne pointed over my shoulder and I looked back to find Medusa Clary (I would plead drunkenness, but honestly, I never cared what these idiots were named) staggering across my lawn, still brushing lit embers out of her hair.

"Good call," I said, and took her legs out from beneath her with a light net. She thumped hard on the ground and I cemented her to the grass with another net before covering the other three in the same. The other female Clary was in particularly bad shape, having caught her cousin/brother/father/lover to the face, but I couldn't tell a difference between how she looked now and how she'd looked before.

"They came here to kill you, didn't they?" Ariadne said, stepping through the gaping hole in the front of our house, rubbing her hands against the arms of her dark suit, which was now covered in dust.

"I doubt they came to play tiddlywinks," I said, dulled by more margaritas than had probably been wise. She was right, after all. They'd come here to kill me, and it was just my good luck that they were so dumb that they thought a frontal assault against me was the best way to settle their grudge. Too bad for them I settled their damned hash.

"Sienna," Ariadne said quietly, connecting dots I didn't really want to connect. "These people … they're—"

"Stupid?" Sirens were blaring in the distance, but I didn't care. *Let the morons wake up,* I sorta prayed. Giving them another dose of hell before the cops came to take them away would be a blessing for me, really.

"Well, yes, obviously, being related to Clyde," Ariadne said, "but that's not what I meant." She hesitated.

"What did you mean?" I slurred my words, and she frowned at me. "What? Don't judge. I've hard a had day. Or had a hard day. Something."

"The government," Ariadne said, choosing her words carefully, "they just … emptied the Cube."

"I damned well know that, Ariadne," I said, impatient. I looked at my hand and found my knuckles bloody and covered in ash. I also had rings of fire burned through my clothing where I'd been forced to torch my way through Medusa's hair. "I was watching it on TV before the Tweedle-fricking-moron family circus came busting in. What about it?"

She took a slow breath as the sirens got closer and closer, and in the distance tires squealed as the cops came charging in, ready to sort out this disturbance in suburbia. I belched and the strong aroma of margarita came up, flooding its way through my nose and burning my nostrils. Ariadne looked a little put off then steadied herself, as if recapturing the thought she'd had before I so rudely interrupted her. "They came running right away … as soon as they got out, didn't they?"

"Because they're idiots, yes," I said, brushing the dust off my clothes and ignoring the burn holes. Maybe a seamstress could fix them; what did I know about tailoring?

"But there are more," she said.

"Yes, there are always more idiots, it's an iron law of the universe, I'm afraid—"

"I mean," Ariadne said, so firmly that I couldn't help but look at her as she spoke, "there are more metas with a grudge against you, Sienna." She swallowed, and I could see it work its way down her thin throat like she'd swallowed a cherry. "Ones that aren't as stupid or bullish as the Clarys. Ones that are smart, and calculating, and clever, who won't just come running the moment the cell door opened for them."

My brow furrowed as I stared at her. She was starting to make sense, but I was just a little too drunk to be able to put it together. "Wait ... what are you saying?"

"I'm saying ..." she swallowed heavily again, and I could almost taste the fear wafting off her beneath that dignified perfume she wore like a cloud to repel people, "... that the Clarys probably aren't the last people with a grudge who are about to try to kill you.

"They're the first."

9.

"I thought we were done for the day," Augustus grouched as he and Kat filed into the conference room in our Eden Prairie offices. There wasn't a sign out front, but we were a registered detective agency in addition to being for hire to whichever state of the union wanted to pay us to deal with their meta problems. Hell, we'd even done a few freebies for local municipalities that couldn't get their state to pay us. "You know, after we let those cats out of the bag from last night."

"I don't think you're allowed to call people 'cats' unless you want this to turn into a seventies blaxploitation flick," Reed said seriously, leaning back in his chair at a forty-five degree angle.

"Well, that's racist," Augustus said, slumping into his own chair with a grunt. "Also, this office being way the hell out in suburbia is, too. Could you not pick a place closer to downtown and campus? Not that I don't enjoy Minneapolis rush hour, but—wait, no, I don't enjoy Minneapolis rush hour. And I was raised in Atlanta, so I know a little something about rush hour."

"Hi everybody," Kat said, breezing in from behind Augustus. Her arms were laden with shopping bags, causing Ariadne to frown. I wondered idly where she'd been shopping, then remembered I didn't really care what Kat did in her off time. "What's going on?" She offloaded the bags with a thump, telling me there was more weight to them than seemed obvious. Sometimes even I forgot that in spite of her stick-figure size, Kat was a meta, with all the strength that came with that.

"Sienna was nearly assassinated by the Clary family a little over an hour ago," Ariadne said, a little more theatrically than I thought the circumstances warranted.

"What?" Reed leaned forward so fast I heard the chair's spring break. He hadn't even asked what was going on before Kat and Augustus had arrived for our little impromptu meeting, probably figuring it was a tactical assessment of the sort I tended to call when we were hunting a fugitive or something.

"I think you're overselling it with the 'nearly,'" I said. "They really didn't get that close to succeeding at anything other than putting a massive hole in my wall."

"What happened?" Augustus asked.

"Yes, what happened?" Kat asked, leaning forward with what smelled like a false sense of worry, like she was playing to cameras that weren't even here. She seemed to be doing that a lot more lately, now that she was filming her stupid show again.

"It was pretty simple, really," I said, cutting off Ariadne before she had a chance to make things sound worse. "They came, I saw, I beat the ever-loving shit out of their hillbilly asses. Took less than five minutes. NBD."

"It's a big deal when newly released prisoners make your house their first stop," Reed said, his voice heavy with concern.

"Not when they get knocked flat in less time than it takes me to shovel the driveway and walk." I hated doing that. Even with meta strength and speed.

"Aww, hell, it's gonna start snowing again soon, isn't it? This town …" Augustus seemed lost in his own thoughts.

"Sienna was nearly murdered tonight," Reed said, looking accusingly down the table at him.

"I kinda doubt it, based on her reaction," Augustus said. "Did you even have to heal yourself?" This he directed at me.

"No," I said.

"She's reaching peak badass, I'm not worried about her,"

Augustus said, waving it off. "Some fool messes with her, they're heading for the morgue. But she ain't the only one with enemies that got out today, and not all of us are nearly as cool as Sienna Nealon."

"Hey, I didn't kill the Clarys," I said. "They're all in custody again, and this time we have fresh charges to make stick. Attempted murder, assault, destruction of property—"

"What do you figure they'll set the bail at?" Reed murmured darkly.

"They were living on fraudulently obtained Social Security when we found them, so I imagine wherever it's set, it'll probably be out of reach," I said. "If they're not denied outright. This is a case of attempted murder, after all."

I heard the front doors open and someone came in just out of sight of the conference room doors. I knew the footsteps, though, the stride and cadence. Our visitor was wearing boots, and in the silence as we waited I could tell he was walking in a measured way.

"Hey, Hampton," Reed called, looking unamused and not taking his eyes off me.

Jeremy Hampton appeared at the doorway, looking formal and professional. "Sorry if I'm late. I had to make my way over from Woodbury, and—"

"The traffic, am I right?" Augustus asked. "It's hellacious."

"It is rush hour," Hampton said, taking a seat at the far end of the table. "If you don't like this, I suggest you never live in Chicago." He gave me a momentary glance, cool and neutral, which was how he always acted toward me in these meetings. "What did I miss?"

"The Clary family used their first day of freedom from the Cube to try and kill Sienna," Reed said, gaze still anchored on me.

Hampton's eyebrow moved upward almost imperceptibly and I caught the hint of worry. "And are they—"

"They're in custody, with bodily harm aplenty to keep them occupied and warned off," I said.

"That's good," Hampton said stiffly. I knew him well enough to recognize the seeds of concern starting to sprout in his head. "That they're out of play."

"Yeah, well, there's a pretty big list that's not out of play," Reed said, leaning back again, chair clacking since he'd broken the spring. "I figured we were just going to do a threat assessment—"

"Before we get into that," Hampton said, "I caught a look at a couple of unsavory characters malingering outside. I figured them for fanboys, but maybe we should—"

I was out of my seat before anyone else and out the door a second later. Our office door opened right to the outside of the old brick and glass office building, which was situated on a pretty major road in Eden Prairie, Minnesota. It was convenient for the mall and lots of restaurants, which was the main reason we'd gone for it.

Also, there was an ice cream parlor next door, which might have had a little something to do with my approval of this office location.

I cast a look down the covered-over sidewalk that stretched between our office door and the ice cream parlor down the way. Picnic tables were set out under the overhang, a perfect place to sit and eat ice cream on hot summer days. The summer days were pretty well past by now, though, which was why I was surprised to see three guys sitting outside, two of them letting off a peal of laughter at something the other one said. Not one of them had a cone in hand.

And I knew all three of them from the Cube.

10.

Normally, when I'm attacking an enemy with superior numbers, I wouldn't tend to announce myself, I'd just sweep in and wipe out my enemies. In this case, though, I couldn't help it.

"Thunder Hayes," I said, and one of the guys craned his neck around to look at me. He had dark, dark eyes. "Bronson McCartney." Another turned to look at me, this one with broad shoulders and a long yet still pug nose that made him look like a bear. "And Louis Terry." The last guy was sitting facing me, opposite the other two. He had bright blond hair that I might have assumed was bleached, except I knew for a fact he'd been sitting his ass in jail for the last few years and never had access to bleach. I thundered up to the three of them, stopping about ten paces away, my hackles all up.

"You best back off, girl," Hayes rumbled. "We're honest citizens now, and we ain't done nothing to you."

"Yeah," Bronson rumbled, looking a little like the bear I knew he could turn into with his meta powers. He was a skinchanger, with the ability to take animal form. "We're just sitting here all peaceable, having some ice cream."

"I don't see any ice cream," I said. Now I had another reason for regretting getting an office right next to an ice cream parlor, and it wasn't just because of my ass anymore.

"We haven't gotten it yet," Terry chimed in. He was an oily son of a bitch, hair all slicked back. He reminded me of a meth-head version of Draco Malfoy, but lacking any of the charm Tom Felton gave the character. "We're just sitting here enjoying our evening before we get our ice cream." He stuck his nose forward and grinned, displaying uneven teeth. They'd been a lot straighter before I met him. "You gonna start something with us, Warden?"

"She ain't a warden of anything, anymore," Hayes said, watching me with those furtive eyes. Even if I'd been blind, I could have smelled the trouble he brought with him. "Now she's a regular citizen, just making her way in the world."

"Your regular citizen has a gun at the small of her back," McCartney said with a snort. Normally when people pick out that I'm armed, they at least have the decency to worry about what that might mean for the continued integrity of their brain tissue, since 9mm hollowpoints plus my deadshot accuracy play all kinds of hell with one's ability to maintain an intact skull. That McCartney seemed to have little care for the fact I was carrying …

Well, it sent a chill up my back that had nothing to do with the autumn weather.

"We know enough to stay on the right side of the law this time," Hayes said, taunting me. "Which is why we're just minding our business here instead of doing anything hostile." He smirked. "We're just customers of a neighborhood business. You're not gonna shoot us for that … are you?" The smirk widened, and it irked the shit out of me that he knew I wouldn't do it.

I was on legally shaky ground if I provoked any of these three, and for all I knew, they were ready for it and would make it very difficult for me to look like anything but a bully. I could practically smell a trap, like they were here just to raise my ire and see what happened. As far as plans went, this was not among the very brightest—pissing off Sienna Nealon was probably a category of risk on insurance underwriter forms by now—but they weren't among the very brightest of criminals, either.

They were, however, not criminals in the sight of the law at the moment, and if I got all up in their faces … I would be.

"So you're like a neighborhood watch," I said tightly. I

knew Reed, Augustus and Hampton were a few steps behind me. I could pick out their breathing, but they were also giving me a lot of space, maybe because they suspected a trap.

"Exactly," Hayes said, nodding. "We're just sitting here and watching the neighborhood."

"It's a very quiet neighborhood most of the time," I said. "When new parolees aren't hanging around."

"Are you impugning our reputations?" Terry's hand flew to his chest, and he wore a *Well-I-never* look of faux offense that was as transparent as the coincidence of him showing up right here, right now.

"You don't need to worry about us," McCartney said, turning his back on me. "We're not going to start anything with you, Nealon."

"Oh no?" I asked.

"Not us," Hayes agreed. "Like we said ... we're just watching." His dark eyes gleamed. "But I would bet someone else ... some less responsible citizen, for instance—"

"Less upright," Terry tossed in.

"Someone less morally straight," McCartney rumbled.

"—they might be along in the next few days," Hayes said, silkily smooth. "And we'd hate to miss anything ... you know, in our capacity as Neighborhood Watch." He gave me a toothy grin. "And I promise we *will* watch it all happen."

"You get your jollies watching your former fellow inmates getting their clocks cleaned?" I kept my hands by my side. "Because that's what's going to happen. Like your pals the Clarys, for instance—"

"Never heard of 'em," Hayes said.

"Who?" Terry asked.

"Bunch of idiots," McCartney said, breaking the chorus effect and drawing ireful looks from both Terry and Hayes. "What? They were. You both said the same thing—the Clarys don't have a chance, it's Shafer and Borosky that we're—"

Hayes thumped McCartney on the arm, his eyes wide and furious. "You. Idiot."

"Sonofa," I muttered under my breath and promptly turned my back on the table of morons behind me. Reed and the others were waiting, and I shot past them as I made for the door to the office.

"You're not gonna see 'em coming, Nealon!" Hayes shouted after me. "Even with us warning you. Shafer and Borosky are like ghosts! They kill people for a living, and they've gotten real wealthy doin—"

His voice was lost to the heavy glass and walls between us as I entered the conference room where I'd been having my little meeting only minutes before. It was quiet, save for Kat, who was sitting there on her cell phone, chattering away.

"No, I'll probably be back tomorrow—I'll take the first flight to LA and—" She saw the storm in my eyes. "Err ... maybe not. Lemme call you back."

"Who're Borosky and Shafer?" Augustus asked as he slid back into his seat. I heard rather than saw him, because my face was pointed at the wall behind my chair, trying to hide the emotions on my face from the meeting at large.

"I don't know," Ariadne said, and I could hear the frown in her voice, "but they sound familiar, don't they?"

"They should," I said, and I turned. They were standing there, waiting, all in various states of anticipation.

Except Reed. Reed looked like he'd had his blood drained, he was so white in the face. He remembered, of course.

"So who are they?" Augustus said. "Convenience store robbers? Attempted terrorists? I mean, they can't be that badass if no one remembers their names—"

"They're assassins," I said, way more coolly than I felt. "They're the ones who bombed Reed's car ... the ones who nearly killed him."

11.

I panted lightly in the darkness in a hotel room on the St. Paul side of the Twin Cities. Jeremy Hampton rolled over, grunting lightly as his weight left me. I was still mostly dressed and so was he, which was how you had to do these things, these nighttime things, when you were a succubus who could steal souls with the touch of your skin.

Staying over in St. Paul had been Jeremy's idea, not mine. It felt like running to me. I lay there in the darkness, sweaty from our exertions, and caught my breath within a few seconds. I was still breathing a little hard, though, because I wasn't happy with any part of what had happened in the last day.

"You got a little rough there," Jeremy said as he got out of bed. He had a pretty soft voice with me, which was a contrast to the drill-sergeant style he used when he was training our civilian SWAT team.

I stared at the ceiling as a car's headlights somehow pushed around the edges of the curtains in order to sweep the room. It illuminated the little bumps of the ceiling, a thousand little molehills, or anthills—something small, almost insignificant, and yet here I was, wasting my time staring at them. "Is that your roundabout way of asking me if this stuff is getting to me?"

"I wouldn't ask that," he said, stripping off his t-shirt. I figured he was about to hit the showers, because that's usually what he did afterward.

"Too personal?" My voice sounded strangely lifeless in my

own ears; I couldn't imagine how it sounded to his.

He let out a dry chuckle. "Hardly. No, it's more because when I've gone through post-mission … shit, honestly … I always hated it when they sent in the psych eval brigade to ask stupid questions about how I felt."

"Was that in the FBI?" I asked.

"SpecOps. FBI HRT was a little less hairy than the SOCOM stuff—most of the time."

"You didn't let many bad guys get away in the Hostage Rescue Team, did you?" I asked.

"Not get away, no," he said and stopped. I could see the outside light shining in across his muscled chest. He'd dropped trow, shedding his boxers and peeling off his socks. "But they didn't all end in violence and blood, either. Sometimes we could talk 'em down with a good negotiator."

"I have a feeling this isn't going to end with anyone talking down the assassins that are coming after me—or my brother." My voice got even tighter. "Or … someone else." I pushed against the springs of the hotel bed and they squealed in protest. Damned ice cream. "You shouldn't be here with me right now."

There was dry amusement in his answer. "We're pretty hidden right now, I doubt anyone's gonna find us all the way over here."

"It's St. Paul, not the other side of the world," I said, still staring at the ceiling. There was a name on my mind, and it was that name that worried me a lot more than Borosky or Shafer. "If they're marginally competent, they can find me." I only hoped Reed had taken my advice and gotten Dr. Perugini out of the damned state. He was supposed to take her anywhere, anywhere at all, for at least the weekend and possibly longer. He'd been a little reluctant to abandon me until I'd made the point that Perugini was a lot more vulnerable than I was. Then he'd paled and gone off to do my bidding.

A stray thought pried loose a smile. "What?" Hampton asked. Now he was fully nude, all silhouette and shadow. I was throwing a few glances here and there as he started toward the bathroom.

"I was just thinking how much easier life would be if everyone would just … do what I told them to." I chuckled at myself.

"Yeah, that's some real totalitarian stuff there," Hampton said.

"It does have a little bit of an Anakin Skywalker in the prequels vibe, doesn't it?"

"I don't think I know what you mean by that reference," Hampton said, caught in shadow. "But, uh … yeah. I'm glad you laughed, because the serious side of that? Yikes."

"I don't actually want to control anyone else," I said, picking up his pillow and cramming it against my side. It felt like a soft person leaned there, a substitute for him while I waited for him to finish showering and rejoin me. "I barely want to control myself—which is at least half my problem."

"Well, that's the difference between you and other people with power, then," Hampton said, sounding like he was about to wax philosophical on me. "You could be a great totalitarian, but you don't really want to do it."

"There are some who would disagree with you."

"I'm not saying you're not a heavy hammer of authority," he said. "Some authority is not a bad thing. It's what holds society together, the lawful use of power along pre-agreed means in the form of laws."

"Ugh, another lecture," I said, a little teasing.

"Stop me if you've heard this one—"

"I've heard it, or some variant on it, from my brother, I'm sure. He has a whole series on politics—"

"Fine," Hampton said lightly, taking my ribbing without getting mad about it. "I'll just say this, then—you may occasionally cross the line into being an authoritarian—which is to say you land the hammer on people who step out of your perceived lines pretty hard sometimes. But you don't show the interest in total control of them that a totalitarian would."

My eyes buzzed side to side in the darkness. "Uhh … that doesn't seem like much of a distinction."

"It's a really important one, actually." He sat down on the bed next to me, rocking the flimsy, too-thin mattress as he rested his bare buttock on it. When he got up, I planned to give him a slap. "Authoritarians want you to follow the rules. Strict rules, in the case of a real authoritarian, too strict, ones that make society … tyrannical. Maybe unlivable. But a totalitarian … they want you to be a puppet. A slave. No action taken without their leave, nothing done without their grace."

I didn't really see it. "Yes, okay, well, I guess I'm just mildly controlling instead of totally controlling, then. I'm sure people will really appreciate that difference, especially these lugs that seem to have it out for me—"

"Did you mean what you said a minute ago?" There was a subtle but distinct change in the tone of his voice.

"About what?"

"You really want me to leave?" he asked. He sounded pretty even about it, not offended, just quiet.

"Maybe," I said.

"I'm eyes wide open on this, okay?" He moved in the dark, the light shifting across his flawless skin. "I know what metas are, and I know what they can do."

"There's a difference," I said with a sigh, "between knowing one and facing one. Having a meta use their speed to zip into your retention zone and rip your pistol right out of your hands, taking a finger with it? Drives the point right home."

There was a long moment of silence in the darkness. "… Has that ever happened to you?"

I sat up, pulling my shirt down over my bra. "No. I've done it to others."

"Ah," he said. "That explains it."

"It really doesn't," I said. "Look … I've lost a human boyfriend to metahumans before. I'm growing fond of you and I don't …" I brushed sweaty hair off my forehead. "I know you're a tough guy. A real badass—"

"I don't think I'd hold much appeal for you if I wasn't."

"Probably not," I said. "But either way … a small army of people who have a grudge against me and a shit-ton more physical strength and a multiplicity of nasty powers just got out of jail today. And I don't know what they're all up to."

"I can see why you'd worry," he said. "So … again … do you want me to go? Because I could be of use here, but—"

"I want you to go," I said, swallowing hard. "In a gig where we get hired to take out the bad guys, we have the advantage of coming at them. In this … they're coming at us, and I wouldn't put it past any of them to go low—right where they figure it'll hurt me most."

"Well, I don't want to be your Achilles heel," he said, getting to his feet. I tried to keep my gaze up, up at his shadowy face, but failed. "I'll take a little vacay for a bit. Maybe … see Wisconsin Dells. But if you need me—"

"I know your number," I said, and caught a hint of a smile in the darkness before he disappeared into the bathroom and closed the door. I knew he wouldn't outstay his welcome; Jeremy was the most reasonable guy I'd ever dated—

Hey, Zack said.

"Let's not candy-coat this, Zack," I said, "you and I had arguments." I spoke to the voice in my head, aloud in the darkened hotel room. "Lots of arguments."

I wasn't unreasonable, though, he huffed.

"You were spying on me for Winter at one point," I said. "That's reasonable?"

Bjorn guffawed in my head. *The instinct for blood is strong. I look forward to the fights to come, the foes yet to fall. You should kill them.*

"I'm trying to play nice," I said.

A losing strategy against these odds, Roberto Bastian said. *You used to play smarter than this.*

"It's not a game anymore," I said. "Screw up before, I had the authority of the government behind me. Screw up now … they're against me. Scott Byerly's whole goal in life is to arrest me." My face felt like a concrete mask. "President Harmon wants me out of the way." A little thought flittered across my mind—but no, he couldn't have had anything to do with this decision. I was no fan of Harmon, but he only had so much sway in Washington, and the SCOTUS ruling had reversed his own policy on meta detentions. This had been his program, through and through, and although I hadn't caught a statement from the White House, I didn't see how he could view this as anything other than a major repudiation of his handling of metahuman justice from the big reveal until now.

You're driving another man away, Eve Kappler said. It sounded suspiciously like crowing.

"Well, there are several billion of them yet, so I suppose I don't feel starved for choice." That was a lie.

Not too many lining up to date you, though, she sniffed. *Especially of quality.*

"Zack," I said, "aren't you offended by that?" I didn't really care what she'd said, I kinda just wanted her to leave me alone.

I'm dead and thus exempt from standing in that line anymore, Zack said, but he sounded a little miffed. *I can't really disagree with her. This Hampton guy,* his tone got tighter, *isn't bad. Better than some of the other guys who have come and gone in the last few ye—*

"I think my dead ex just made an oblique comment about my sex life," I said, staring off into the darkness, more amused than irritated. "This isn't the moment to talk about relationship goals."

What do you want to talk about, then? Wolfe entered the conversation. He tended to do that, play lead in the arguments in my head. It was hard to tell whether he was sucking up to me or just fancied himself in charge of the other souls who occupied my skull, like he had seniority because he'd been living there longest.

"I want to talk about killing these assholes before they cause me problems," I said, a little emotion causing me to shiver. "But I can't."

You did with Nadine Griffin, Wolfe said, just teasing a little.

"This is different," I whispered.

She was guilty, Wolfe said. *They're guilty. No difference.*

"And if I get caught ... I'll be guilty, too," I said, imagining a line between me and them. I may have crossed that line a few times before, most recently with the aforementioned Nadine Griffin, but I had purer motives for what I'd done to her. Lives were being destroyed by that woman, and no one could seem to trip her up. So far, the morons who had come after me had been easily tripped, beaten, and subdued. "I'm not doing it," I said, dismissing the thought. "Let them come to me. If it gets heated and I have to end one of them in self-defense … then that's what I'll do. But it has to be a righteous kill."

All my kills were righteous, Wolfe said, and I could almost see his grin in the dark.

"Shut up, Wolfe," I said, but I wondered if maybe I was irritated at him because he sounded just a little too close to justifying himself the way I was doing.

12.

Reed

"We have to go," I said, looking into her brown eyes. The skeptical look I was receiving in return didn't exactly fill me with confidence that I was going to have much luck with this line of argument. Which was funny, because when my sister had told me to get the hell out of Dodge, I'd almost fallen over myself agreeing with her. Not for my sake, but for that of the lovely woman in front of me.

"Why?" Dr. Isabella Perugini asked. She was sitting comfortably on the couch in our apartment, her copy of this week's *National Enquirer* spread open across her beautiful, olive complexioned legs. She was wearing a very short robe, the sort that might normally have given me ideas about something other than fleeing the greater metro area, but right now, getting the hell out of town—and not for a romantic getaway—was the only thing on my mind.

"Because these assassins are out," I said, "the ones that blew up Baby—my car."

"I know who Baby is," she gave me a poisonous look, the one she directed at me when she thought I was being stupid. I recognized it from its all-too-frequent employment. "How do you know these assassins will even come after you? Do you have some vendetta between you?"

I pondered the answer to that one carefully. "Well," I finally said, "I can't say for sure that they're going to consider the contract to kill me unfulfilled, but how badly do you want to find out?"

"You are so dramatic." Isabella made a scoffing noise in the back of her throat. "You say your sister is dramatic, I say you both are. It is a family trait." She leafed through a page of her *Enquirer* without looking at it, then brought her brown eyes back up to me, all warm and showing the barest edge of worry. "This troubles you, these convicts being released?"

"The Clarys already made a run at Sienna," I said. "Three other guys are just sitting outside the office, stalking and waiting. They said Borosky and Shafer are keen on revenge. That worries me, since the last time they came at us, I ended up having to regrow my hair."

"You did not look right bald," she agreed, taking a moment to run fingers through my long, dark hair. It wasn't as long as hers, but close. She sighed deeply, disentangling her fingers. "I hate to leave because of something like this. How long might we be gone, if we run from these *stronzi*? And when the next threat comes along? How long will we run then?"

"It's not just any threat," I said. "Remember, Fintan O'Niall and Lorenzo Benedetti were among the guys that released—"

She looked at me with near inscrutability, which I knew by long experience meant she was mad. "I remember well Lorenzo and Fintan, the happy servants of Anselmo the dickless."

Anselmo would not have responded to her favorably for calling him that. Fortunately, he was good and dead. I'd personally made sure he ended up on the ash heap of history. "Well, if you recall, they have something of a grudge against me—or us, possibly—"

The front door burst off its hinges in a storm of wind, as if Lorenzo had timed it for full dramatic effect.

He blew in, dressed all in black and with his Aeolus winds swirling around, knocking pictures off the wall and ripping the drapes off the curtain rod. "I am returned for you, Reed Treston," he said ominously, gliding into the room on a little gust of wind, his bare feet exposed so he could channel his powers through them.

"Where's Fintan?" I asked, rising up and putting myself between him and Isabella.

"I have no need of Fintan," Lorenzo said, hovering there like Sienna, except he was producing gusts while doing so. "Our concerns are our own, and my anger with you is my own—"

I put my head back slightly as I looked at the ceiling, and then rolled my eyes all the way back. "Please, Lorenzo … Hera died years ago. Can you please just get rid of these unresolved issues with a therapist like a normal person? This isn't healthy, dude." I nodded toward the curtains just as the rod ripped off the wall on one side and clanged against the tile floor. "Also, that drapery? It took forever to get her to decide on a freaking color for that. Literally forever. You could have worked through all your mommy issues with Hera in the time I spent in that store."

"I think you should insult your enemies and be wary of insulting your lady," Isabella said from just behind me, and I was suddenly a lot more scared of her than Lorenzo. Actually, there was nothing that sudden about it; it was a fairly constant state.

"I'm not insulting you, dear, but you have a difficult time making decisions, especially about design elements," I said. "I mean, really, it's a cream color. It goes with beige, no prob—"

"I wanted it to tie the room together, and there were issues of the other pieces of decor—"

"I'm just saying, it's a neutral, it—"

"ENOUGH!" Lorenzo said, thrusting a hand toward me and blasting me with a tornado of wind that I dispelled with a wave of the hand.

"—goes with anything," I said. "It felt like you were agonizing over it just for the sake of agonizing, you know? I just don't like to see you get all worked up over—"

"You will die!" Lorenzo said, and he blasted at me again. I dispelled his furious gale once more.

"—it's just not that big a deal. A few shades in either direction and we'd still be good."

Isabella was watching me with wide eyes. "I thought you

were worried about this man."

"Fintan's not with him, so no," I said, barely giving Lorenzo consideration. I was still watching him out of the corner of my eye, but a lot of my angst had died out.

"You will fear me!" Lorenzo shouted, desperate for attention. "When last we clashed, I nearly killed you!"

I half-turned back to him. "When last we clashed … it was a few years ago. I've trained a lot since then. Learned a few things. I've leveled up, Lorenzo. Wanna see?" He stared at me in inchoate rage, trying to summon words, but I kicked at him from halfway across the room. It probably looked funny, until I blasted a gust through the bottom of my foot and my loafer shot off and blew across the room, guided by a couple of minor crosswinds to hit him unerringly in the nose. The snap of bone was pretty loud, and his hands flew up as the blood started to slide down.

I caught the loafer in a crosswind and blew it back around to clap him lightly in the back of the head, right in the occipital notch. Then I brought it around again to slap him in the face. Finally I vortexed it back across the room to land in front of me, and I slipped it back on while he stared at me in impotent fury. "To quote my sister, 'Wrong house,' Lorenzo. Wrong guy."

There was a red mark on his cheek where I'd shoe slapped him, and he held his hand to it. "It is you who have made the error, Reed," Lorenzo said, puffing a little as he pulled his hand away from his red cheek.

That didn't sit well with me. "Oh, really?" I asked. "How is—"

The front window exploded with glass as something leapt through and collided with me before I could do much more than push Isabella back and raise an arm to shield my face. It was a rookie mistake, trusting Lorenzo when he'd said Fintan wasn't with him. He'd seemed so earnestly angry, though, so sure of his ability to take me out solo, I figured he was telling the truth.

I realized, as Fintan the Firbolg collided with me in a frenzy of battle rage, that I had made a terrible, terrible mistake. So much worse even than that time I'd tried wearing skinny jeans because I thought they would make me look cool.

Fintan was atop me a second later, straddling me with all his weight. His flat nose was right in my face, and for a brief and horrible second, I thought he was about to tear my throat out with his teeth. His breath reeked like he hadn't had a meal in a while, and his last one seemed like it might have been the ass of a vulture.

Then my hours and hours of training with Sienna kicked in and I reacted instinctively. We'd trained for these sorts of scenarios, and my sister took a sadistic sort of glee in overpowering me and making me cope with it. I'd never had a sibling who could put my head in the toilet or rub my face in the carpeting until I got rug burn—at least not as a child. I'd had it done to me plenty as an adult, though, when I got my ass regularly handed to me by my little sister.

My shirt rippled as I channeled a powerful gust out through my stomach. It was everything I had, thrown into one good burst, and Fintan shot into the air and smashed into the ceiling, leaving man-shaped cracks. He didn't looked particularly harmed by his flight, but his flat face showed the signs of surprise as he started to come back down, and I greeted him with a fist to the face and another to the gut. Then I kicked him sideways and he slammed into the wall of the living room before he could tear me to pieces.

A gust of wind hit me from the side, and I slid a few feet before I managed to reverse it. My more powerful gust sent Lorenzo crashing into the drywall behind the front door. He folded at the midsection as he went into the wall, his arms and legs sticking out like overgrown weeds in a vegetable patch.

"GRAAARGH!" Fintan shouted, appearing above me again. He wasn't slow, but he seemed to be acting on instinct rather than the more careful calculation I'd learned from my sister pummeling my ass until I started to think during a fight. I blew a gust from my leg and slid in a tight arc around, my shirt gliding on the tile as I took Fintan's legs from beneath him in a sweep. I fired a couple quick gusts from my hand and flipped back to my feet, then shot another that sent him sliding into the baseboard with a crack. Again, it didn't hurt him much, but he did look slightly dazed.

"Sorry," I said to Isabella as I channeled a gust in reverse and pulled Fintan toward me, along with a bookshelf, a dozen heavy books with Italian titles on their spines, and a few pictures that had been hung to give the room a warmer, homier feel. I dodged aside and sent Fintan back out onto the lawn because I was sick of messing up our modest decorating efforts while I was defending myself. "Stay here, I'll be back once they're both dealt with." And with a flick of the hand I shot the recovering Lorenzo out the door in a gust that ripped the front door off its already flagging hinges.

I launched myself out onto the lawn and came down with a gust punch right to Fintan's abdomen. It was a thing I'd been working on, channeling a wind in a tightly focused cone so it hit hard and fast, and on a small amount of surface area. Augustus had given me the idea, using his dirt projections as spears from time to time. I brought another gust punch around and caught Lorenzo beneath the chin as he started to rise. His legs got watery weak and he plopped back to his ass. I could tell he was dazed from the beating, which was a pleasant reversal of what had happened the last time we'd clashed.

I turned back to deal with Fintan, but he was already on his feet. He launched at me, and even though I tried to gust him away, he turned his body enough to deflect it. He slashed along my belly with his fingernails, and a fiery pain cut across my guts. It stunned me, paralyzed me, and my legs gave out from the pain.

Fintan took me to my knees, and then he came and smashed me across the face. My right eye closed involuntarily, stars blew across my field of vision, and I lost a few seconds of my life. When I came back to myself, Fintan hit me again, then again, and I barely felt either blow. I could tell by the way the night rocked around me, my house and the ones across the street swimming into view and then out again, that he was pummeling the hell out of me. I hit the lawn and stared up at the night sky as he railed on me again, and something in the side of my face gave way.

I put a hand up, and he started to come at me again, feral savagery all I could see, and I blew him lightly from the ground, but only a foot or so. I felt like I was floating, too, which was a measure of how bad a shape I must have been in. My hand shook trying to keep him aloft, out of reach, so he couldn't tear me up any more, but I knew this wouldn't last long. He was swimming against the tide of my power, teeth bared, furious, ready to rip me apart the moment his feet touched the earth.

A thundercrack exploded in the quiet suburban night, a flash like lightning preceding the sound by less than a second. Fintan spun in midair, and another crack followed, and another, flashes lighting the sky. Blood flecked my face like a warm rain, and Fintan's belly was open, guts spilling out, horror and anguish lighting his face. Then another thunderclap bellowed forth and Fintan's face disappeared in a shower of blood and bone and muscle, and he went limp as he fell out of my field of vision.

I stared into the dark night for only a moment before Isabella's face came swimming into view. "Oh, Reed," she breathed, sounding terrified in a way that a doctor never should. Doctors were supposed to have seen this and worse, and her lack of professional distance caused my heart to drop. She tossed her shotgun aside and her hands found their way to my face.

"Still … think I'm being … dramatic?" I asked, but I didn't get a chance to see her response before the night faded before me and I lost consciousness.

13.

Sienna

"Reed!" I shouted as I came in for a rough landing on my brother's lawn. Dr. Perugini was crouched over him on the stretcher, ambulance and police lights flashing blue and red and white against the jagged shards of the shattered front window of his house.

I craned my neck to look over the shoulders of the paramedics who were working over my brother, and Perugini gave me a sidelong look as I lifted off the ground again for a second, trying to see his face. When I did, I let out a gasp. I couldn't help it.

"He will be fine," Perugini said brusquely, with her usual lack of sunny disposition.

"But his face—" I said.

"It will heal," she said with more confidence than I felt. It was true that metas could heal all manner of damage done to us, but Reed was an Aeolus, which was not nearly as high on the power scale as I was. I could regrow a burnt-off limb even before I got Wolfe's powers. With Reed, I wasn't really sure what kind of damage he could recover from before scars started forming. "He will need time, though," she said, and the paramedics lifted the gurney up from the ground with a click as it settled at wheeling height.

I cast a look at the mess on the lawn. I saw at least one corpse that I didn't recognize because it was missing a face, but there was another guy all cuffed up and trussed, out like a light. Him I recognized as Lorenzo Benedetti, one of Anselmo Serafini's pieces of Italian trash. Another paramedic was tending to him, and he had an IV going right into Lorenzo's arm. "Is that—" I started to ask.

"He'll be out for a while," the paramedic assured me. Middle-aged guy, no nonsense, gave me a confident look. "We won't chance him waking up before we get him transferred to the Cube."

"So you're going to send him back there?" I asked, and noticed there was a cop lingering pretty close to the prisoner.

"That's the directive," the cop said. His hand was resting on his Glock, ready to pull if Lorenzo moved. Two other cops were standing a little further back, also keeping a wary eye on Lorenzo. "We're just waiting for the feds to show up for transport. District Attorney says they're going to make an example of this guy—plus the others that came after you earlier." The cop rolled his eyes. "Glory hound will probably do it, too."

I kept my mouth shut; a glory hound prosecutor looking to make an example of a meta who had committed a crime didn't sound like a bad thing to me, especially if they were going to lock them up in the Cube until trial. The idea of the Clarys and Lorenzo being kept in a county jail made me sweat. "Who was the last guy?" I asked, nodding at the corpse, which they hadn't even bothered to cover up with a sheet.

"Fintan O'Niall," Perugini answered as the paramedics rolled Reed's gurney away, toward the ambulance. I knew the name, and kicked myself for not connecting it earlier. We'd brought in ol' Fintan when we picked up Anselmo and Lorenzo in Italy. Figured they'd hang together—though now two out of three of them had been pretty much hung separately.

"Reed did a nice job on him," I said, nodding at the shotgun discarded on the lawn. It wasn't like my brother to put rounds in someone. He must have been suitably pissed to go that route.

"Pfffft," Perugini said. "I did that, not him. That is *my* shotgun. He still plays with his piddly little pistol, like drawing in pencil." She waved at the carcass. "I prefer the bold strokes of a paintbrush."

"Oh." Suddenly it all made sense. "You certainly brushed him out."

"He asked for it," Perugini said matter-of-factly. "This fool thinks he can come into our home, threaten us?" She spat on the ground, probably angrier than I'd ever seen her, which was saying something since she had regularly been furious with me throughout our acquaintance.

"Is he well enough to travel in a plane?" I asked, and she glowered at me. "Chartered flight? Private plane? With medical care?"

"Yes," she said, and a little of her suspicion died. "Why?"

"I'm going to have Ariadne charter you a jet out of here," I said, fishing for my phone. "Kat and Augustus will go with you—"

"Leaving you alone?" She raised an eyebrow and the glower made a triumphant return. "I don't think so."

"I'll be fine," I said, pretty sure I wasn't lying. "I want you all out of the way, though, and hidden."

"And who will help you?" she asked. "Reed would not condone this, you see."

"I'll get help if I need it," I said. "But right now I'm worried about the rest of you." I gave the paramedics a look; they were loading Reed into the back of the ambulance. "These people, these prisoners … they know my weak point is the rest of you. They can come at me all day long, like the Clarys did, and it's just going to end in a mess for them. But if they come at you … any of you," I said, nodding at her, and she seemed to take the comment in the spirit I intended it, by softening the glower to a low glare, "they win, even if I perform a colonoscopy with a shotgun on them afterward." I glanced at the body of Fintan again. "Which, I see, you have some experience with."

"It was simple skeet shooting," Perugini said dismissively. "My father taught me when I was young. Reed held him up, and I took him out of the sky like a clay pigeon." She stuck a thin finger in my face. "If you get yourself hurt or killed while he is recovering, he will be most displeased with us both. And he will take this anger out on me, and I will have nowhere to go with it if you die."

"I'll do my best not to die," I said. "Life with a surly, passive-aggressive Reed sounds like a hell I wouldn't wish even on you."

She wagged that thin finger again. Geez. Everything about her was thin. "You had better not."

I nodded once, and she stalked off to the back of the ambulance where she yelled something in Italian at one of the attendants, who just looked at her blankly. "Watch his head, *idiota!*"

"I was, ma'am," the paramedic said, straining to keep polite.

I pulled my phone out and dialed a number. It rang twice before it was answered. "Damn, girl, in the middle of the night? This better not be a booty call."

"You just keep making it weird between us, Veronika," I said. I heard the faint sound of tired laughter through the phone. "I need your help, and damned sure not that kind."

"For pay, I hope, because in spite of how I might tease you, we're not quite to the point in our relationship where favors get traded back and forth yet."

"For pay," I said. "Reed got racked up by a couple parolees, and I'm sending him to San Fran to recover along with the rest of my team. Others might come after him, and I want you to keep an eye on him."

She was pretty quiet for a second. "Damn. Okay. I'm in. But if you've some bucks to spread around, can I recommend—"

"My firm will cover it," I said, already jumping ahead. "They'll cover it all. I want you to have some backup."

"Pretty sure Colin wouldn't mind running picket duty around wherever we're staying, and Phinneus is always up for playing overwatch," she said, all trace of tiredness vanished. "You want me to put it together?"

"Please do," I said. "And Veronika—"

"Don't worry," she said, and I could hear her already moving on the other end. "I'll protect them like they're my very own. No harm will come to them. But I gotta say, I was watching the release ceremony earlier … and that was a lot of fish being let back into the sea. You really think they're gonna come after your brother and your other minions?"

"I very much doubt it," I replied. "I think they're going to come for me."

She drew a long breath through gritted teeth. "Man, I feel bad for those guys."

"You should," I said. "Take care, Veronika."

"I'll take care—and take care of them. Go do your thang, and do us ladies proud."

"You know I will," I said, and hung up on her. "You know I will."

14.

I stayed to watch Lorenzo Benedetti get taken into federal custody, and I ended up getting a show. Lucky me.

The ambulance had cleared off by the time the feds arrived, and they'd even taken ol' Fintan's cold carcass to the morgue by the time the boys from DC showed up. I had hoped it'd just be local FBI guys that would come to do the transport. Them or the marshals.

I was not nearly that lucky, and I knew it the moment the black SUV squealed to a stop and Scott Byerly popped out.

He wore what was fast becoming his new trademark, a grimacing scowl that found me in the darkness immediately, where I was standing at the edge of a circle of the local cops, entertaining them with stories of past collars. I had them laughing about this jackass I had run across in Florida who'd fled into the swamp on foot when Scott came out of the darkness, stalking toward me, Guy Friday a few steps behind him, and a hush fell over my new friends in the Eden Prairie PD.

"Well, well, well," Guy Friday said, speaking through his gimp mask. "What do we have here?"

"Have you asked me that before?" I watched him with a practiced indifference. "Don't you ask me that every time?"

"I keep hoping the answer will be different," Friday said smugly. He cracked a smile; Scott did not.

"What we have here," I said, gesturing to Benedetti, who was still IV'd up with tranquilizers, "is today's catch, fresh from the Mediterranean by way of the Cube. He's been prepared with a meat tenderizer, lightly air dried, and is now suitable for transport to the cell block from whence he so recently came."

"Hilarious," Scott pronounced sounding like a surly teenager.

"Well, I was just going for original per Friday's request, but thanks," I said. "Tell me—why are you suddenly my stalker ex?"

Scott looked at me with dry heat, smoky eyes looking like his power was fire, not water. "Oh, I don't know. Because you stole my memories and you're a killer?"

There was a stunned silence in my little circle of new friends. "But what have I done *lately*?" I asked, and one of the cops snorted. They all broke out in laughter a second later. Even Guy Friday smirked, and not smugly, for once.

"Oh, you think murder is funny, do you?" Scott shot back at them, and the cops quieted pretty fast.

"I didn't murder anyone," I lied, rolling my eyes. "I kill in self-defense—"

"Your self needs a lot of defending," Scott snapped.

"Because these big mean boys keep trying to hurt me," I said, playing a little sulky and wounded, "and no big, strong man will come and save the day for me." I put a finger on my lip, pouting—like an ass, and making my voice sound like a little child as I went. "Whatever should a little girl do in such a cwuel, cwuel world?"

That did it for the cops, they burst into laughter again and started to walk off. Knees were slapped, chortles were had, Guy Friday let out a guffaw or two, and Scott just got redder and redder. He waited until the officers had wandered away, leaving me standing next to Lorenzo with Scott glowering at me and Friday lurking over his shoulder, about half pumped-up into his muscled form. "You think it's hilarious how you've gotten away with everything?"

"I haven't gotten away with anything, Scott," I sighed. He looked like he was going to stroke out right there in front of me. "Also, you're here for this criminal," I pointed at Lorenzo, "not me, since I had nothing at all to do with this incident."

"But you had a little incident of your own earlier, didn't you?" Friday asked.

"Why, yes," I said, in mock dismay, "I was the tragic victim of a home invasion perpetrated by a gang of ne'er-do-wells that just so happened to be paroled this very day. Why, I think I should sue the government for releasing them, because they seem to have put me into harm's way—yet again—but I doubt the Supreme Court is going to be very receptive to my case."

"Seems unlikely they'll be sympathetic," Friday agreed.

"They can join the club," Scott said, high voice an octave higher. He sounded like he was in pain from this whole thing. I felt a little bad for him. But not that bad, since the last time we'd met he'd admitted he wanted to smash my face in with a sledgehammer.

"Go on," I said, "say it."

He froze, face losing a shade of red. "Say what?"

"Warn me that you're watching me," I said, letting out a slow sigh. "That you're dogging my footsteps. That I ought to be careful, because if I so much as step outta line, you're gonna *get me*." I tried to make the last part sound comical. "Oh, and just ignore that I delivered those four home invaders back to you alive and in working order, because that cuts against the grain of your 'Sienna's a murderer' profile."

"Yeah, why didn't you kill them?" Friday asked. "It would have been self-defense, easy."

"I'm glad you asked, Friday," I said sweetly, then glared at Scott. "Because I'm trying not to kill people anymore. It's this whole new-leaf thing I'm trying to turn over. Not that anyone seems to notice."

"I bet Nadine noticed," Scott said with pure venom.

I didn't smile. "I'm sure she did, wherever she is. Skiing in Switzerland, probably. Did you ever get in trouble for sleeping with the object of an FBI investigation, by the way?"

"Allegedly," Scott said through clenched teeth.

"Oh, sweetie," I said, "'alleged' doesn't hold any water between the two of us, remember? That benefit of the doubt thing you refuse to extend to me?"

"You will go down," Scott said, leaning in close to me, breath on my ear.

"Not on you," I said tightly, "not anymore."

"Oohhhhhh," Friday crowed like a locker room reject. "She smoked you, bro! That was pure ownage. Pwnage, I think they call it."

"Shut up, Friday," Scott said, ashen and near whispering now. "Get Benedetti, and let's get out of here." He turned hateful eyes on me once again, and I had to try hard not to blanch at the sight of him, of all people, looking at me that way. "You *will* pay for what you've done."

"I've been paying for everything I've done since the first time I saved this city," I said bitterly. "I've lost lovers, friends, my parents, people I've cared about, and some morons just turned loose a jail filled with people who are way more violent and pissed off at me than you are. If you think anything you have to threaten me with comes close to the shit I've dealt with all my life up until this very moment, Scott—" I rose off the ground, looking down on him as I hovered above him, "—you're kidding yourself, rich boy. Do your worst." And I left him there, red-faced and sputtering, and soared off into the air where he couldn't follow.

15.

"Where are you?" I asked the moment J.J. picked up the phone, the air whistling past my face as I soared across the sky. Night had fallen over the Twin Cities, and both Minneapolis and St. Paul were lit up ahead of me, dual skylines glowing with a million little lights.

"In a secret location," J.J. said, voice lowered to a hushed whisper, "where no one can find me."

I hung up on him and veered southeast, flying just below the speed of sound. I stopped when I hit Burnsville, dropping just south of the I-35 merge. I went low, following the GPS on my phone until I ended up in a neighborhood of duplexes, and dropped on a front porch of a grey one that had a lit front window. I checked the house number just to be sure, then stepped up on the porch and rang the doorbell.

A girl opened it a few seconds later, her hair black at the top and pink all the way down to her jawline, where it ended. It was a cute little bob, longer at the front of her face and getting progressively shorter until it reached scalp-length at the back of her head. She had a tiny little piercing in her nose and was wearing a tight, black, mid-riff baring tank top and baggy jeans that were flared at the ankles and really loose. It was a cool look, actually, and she maintained a jaded expression as she said, "Yes?" with just the right note of politeness.

"I need to talk to J.J.," I said.

J.J.'s head popped out from behind a door just behind her

to the left. "What the deuce?" he asked, his jaw hanging low. "How did you find me?"

"I've known for a long time you have a girlfriend," I said, nodding at the girlfriend in question, who was an expert at keeping a neutral expression. "Nice to meet you, Abigail. I'm Sienna."

"Yeah, I know," she said. "Hope you don't mind if I don't shake your hand."

"Smart girl," I said, and she stepped aside to let me in. "You know what's going on?" I asked him.

"Centipede Reed is headed for the hospital, then San Fran," J.J. said, emerging from the doorframe wearing Pokemon boxers and a white t-shirt stained with orange around the belly. I detected—with my meta sense of smell—Cheetos residue, but I decided to take the high road and say nothing about this. The aroma of Monster energy drinks was also in the air. Yuck. I preferred Red Bull when I needed a kick. "Ariadne's private plane charter kicked a flag I had to prevent fraud on the agency accounts."

"I think you should go with them," I said, and then looked at Abigail of the pink hair and worrisome lack of judgment in men. "Both of you, if you want."

"I'd like to fly in a private jet," Abigail said nonchalantly.

"You're worried about us," J.J. said, sounding a little sweet about it. "You think these hapless losers will really be able to dig me out through Abigail?"

"The hapless losers, no," I said, because his assessment of many of the Cube's newly released prisoners was dead on. "But they're not all hapless losers, and we don't know where all of them are."

"You're afraid of Cassidy," he said.

He said it, finally giving voice to what I'd been thinking all along. "She's more dangerous with a keyboard and an internet connection than anyone other than you or Jamal," I said. "And she will not hesitate to put any of you in the path of people who mean to cause me harm. The floodgates are open, and until I sort out who's going to make the most of their second chance and who's going to screw it up ... I don't want to take any chances of my own with your lives."

"That's so sweet," Abigail said. She finally broke the stoic look to give J.J. a questioning one. "You never said she was sweet. You said she was—"

"I don't need to hear—" I started.

"We shouldn't get into—" J.J. said hastily.

"Right," Abigail said, heeding both our warnings as I lowered my gaze to admire her choice in wood flooring and a cheap rug at the entry. "Uhm. Yeah. We should go, huh?"

"That's uh … a good idea," J.J. said, nodding. "I can pack in like five—"

"Good," I said, and Abigail nodded, too. "I want to escort you guys to the airport. Ariadne said the plane would be standing by, so … I want to make sure everyone gets on it, and that I see you all off to a safe distance."

"How far is safe?" Abigail asked with a frown.

"Middle of South Dakota seems reasonable," I said. "None of these people can fly, but I'll feel better knowing J.J. is on board, in case the plane is, uh … hackable, I guess?"

"It shouldn't be," J.J. said, smiling. "But I gotcha covered. I'll go get my stuff. Abby, dear?" He smiled at her, and she headed off down the hallway with some urgency.

"She seems nice," I said, standing awkwardly at the door.

J.J. seemed to know what I was thinking. "It's gonna be okay, Sienna. You're gonna beat these guys. This is what you do."

I forced a smile. "I know. But I'll feel a lot better once you're all out of here, and safely under the protection of Veronika and company."

"Because it lets you do what you need to do without worrying about the rest of us?" he asked, probing just a little farther than I was comfortable with. "Because it gives you … license to … do your thing?" The inference was unmistakable. 'My thing' was code for death.

"Let's hope I don't have to do 'my thing,'" I said softly. It was a feeling of war within myself, a cold dread, as J.J. nodded and withdrew into the room off the hall. It was also very strange; I hadn't hesitated to kill, not for a long time.

The stakes were high until these people—these people I actually cared about—were out of the sniper's scope.

Then, with only my own life on the line, maybe this itch would go away, and I could avoid becoming what Scott kept accusing me of.

The monster that I worried I truly was, deep inside.

16.

Augustus

"I'm gonna miss so much class," I said, sighing as I crammed a half dozen shirts into a gym bag. Night was still in effect outside the windows of my downtown apartment, but you could see some of the taller Minneapolis buildings out the windows—the IDS Tower loomed large, but because I was on the corner, you could see the Wells Fargo Center and the Foshay, as well, but barely.

My pad was dope as hell. I just wished I got to spend more time here.

"Aren't they pretty forgiving about that?" Kat asked. She poked her head into my bedroom, looking around, maybe admiring the view. "I mean, you're kind of a superhero. You'd think they'd give you some leeway."

"They give me some leeway," I said, rolling up a pair of jeans and cramming them in the bag. I put another pair in for good measure. Fancy jeans. The new job at the agency paid really well. Enough that I wasn't exactly living in a dorm room. "But I still need to understand the material, you know. And between all the work we're doing, and the travel for the job, and all the classes I've been taking …" I mopped my forehead and found it sweaty, no surprise. I'd been running around since Sienna had called and told me to scoot. "It's a lot, you know? A lot of pressure."

"Oh, I understand," Kat said, bopping her way into my room. I could tell she was just looking around innocently, but it gave my blood a second of chill thinking Kat Forrest—*the* Kat Forrest, metahuman sex symbol and reality TV star—was in my freaking bedroom, y'all. If Taneshia could have seen this, well …

Actually, it would have been really bad if Taneshia had seen it, innocent as it was.

Kat was just kind of lingering, looking at some of the textbooks I'd crammed into the shelves. She ran her finger down the spine of one of my Biology 101 texts. I shivered a little and hurriedly zipped my bag. Anything I didn't remember to bring, I could just buy once we got to Cali. It wasn't like they didn't have stores, or I didn't have a credit card with lots and lots of room to charge. "We should go."

"Okay," Kat said, shrugging like it didn't matter one way or the other to her. "I had a hired car bring me over, but Sienna said you were going to drive to the airport in Eden Prairie?"

"Yeah, I got this." And I ushered her out the door, locking it behind me.

When we got to the elevator, we waited in the slick hallway for only a few seconds before it dinged its arrival. Kat looked around solemnly, taking it all in, like there were really deep thoughts going on. It made me wonder what she was thinking about, and then she said, "I'm hungry. Do you think we can stop for pizza on the way to the airport?"

Maybe they weren't that deep after all. But with a booty like homegirl had, who needed deep thoughts?

"There's probably food on the plane," I said as we got into the elevator. "We should wait to eat." That sucker sped its way down to the garage below.

"I guess," Kat said, again sounding pretty indifferent. "I was planning to go back to SoCal tomorrow—or later today, now, I guess." She looked at the screen of her phone. "Yeah. I can't believe it's already tomorrow. I miss Pacific time. It feels like you have more time, you know? Because—"

The elevator door dinged open and I looked out on the well-lit but empty garage. "Mmhmm," I said, and put a light hand on her back to guide her out of the elevator. My car was parked just ahead, a brand new BMW 500 Series. Kat didn't say anything about it as she got in the passenger side; she was obviously used to much better. I tossed my bag in the back seat and started it up. It purred. I'd toyed with giving it a name, like Reed had done with his Challenger, but I was too self-conscious. Naming a car was kind of stupid. Plus, this was just a lease.

I sped out of the garage, hitting the button to open the door as I approached and zipping out into the night. I made a turn onto the road, and headed for I-35W. I made a couple turns, watching my rearview mirror the way Hampton had instructed us to, looking for tails. Kat had the sun visor down and was checking her makeup in the mirror when I spotted it.

"Aw, hell," I muttered to myself.

"I know, it's impossible to find a color that matches my skin tone," Kat said. "I have to go to have this specialty stuff done at—"

"Not what I meant," I said, making another turn, this time onto Hennepin, just to confirm. I managed to make it a block before the same damned pair of headlights turned right behind me. "We've got a tail."

"Oh?" Kat put the visor back up and turned around in her seat. "I wonder if it's paparazzi? They follow me a lot," she sort of gushed. It would have been endearing if I didn't seriously doubt that was the case this time.

"I don't think this is paparazzi."

"Trust me," she said, eyes gleaming.

"It's not that I don't trust you," I said, "it's more that we're under threat right now, and I expect we're being followed by people that mean us harm, not ones that want to snap a few pics of you doing the nasty in a car with a stranger."

She stared straight ahead. "Ratings have been down, you know. Ever since I pissed off Taggert by kicking his ass off the production. Maybe getting caught doing something a little dirty could spark some controversy, move the dial back up." She looked right at me, and put on a sweet, dangerously seductive smile. "Say … you wouldn't want to—"

The image of my girlfriend shooting lightning from her

fingertips flashed through my mind. "NO."

I ran the next red light and the car behind me did the same. "Paparazzi do that all the time," Kat said, completely unconcerned. She looked like she was about ready to start filing her nails.

I ditched my plan to get on 35W and sped up as I got on 94 heading west. The headlights followed, the motion of the car calm and controlled. Whoever was behind me was taking it real easy, not even having to put up a lot of effort.

"Who the hell would be following me?" I mumbled, my eyes more fixed on the rearview than the interstate in front of me as I merged onto 94 toward the Lowry tunnel. The interstate was pretty damned quiet this time of night, only a couple of tractor trailers and a small car in sight.

"They're clearly following me," Kat said, tossing her hair. It hypnotized me for a minute, not gonna lie.

"How's a paparazzi supposed to know it's you in this car?" I asked, still watching behind us as I switched lanes. The tunnel was just ahead, and I moved right, figuring I'd get on 394 West and just follow it to 494 South all the way to Eden Prairie and the airport rendezvous. "It's dark as hell out here, and they were on us as we were leaving my building." I shook my head. "Naw. This is something else. This is the trouble Sienna was warning us about."

"Sienna sees enemies in her underwear drawer," Kat scoffed. "Which makes total sense, because she wears granny panties, and they are the enemy of sexiness."

I jerked up straight in my seat, appalled as hell. "Ugh! Why you need to be hitting me with that imagery right now?"

Kat gave me a knowing look. "Like you've never noticed when she bends over real far."

Maybe I had, but having only seen the waistband of whatever she was wearing, I wouldn't have been able to say for sure what she had going on below. Kat was probably not wrong, but still, I didn't need to be thinking about Sienna's undies right now any more than I needed Kat trying to get me in trouble with Taneshia. "Y'all people are more trouble for me than—" I hit the exit ramp to 394 and went hard on the curve, speeding up as soon as I was past the worst of it, my eyes anchored on the rearview again as I shot forward past the HOV exit.

The car behind us sped up, too, and seemed to floor it. I heard the roar of a muscle car's engine, and it didn't take more than a few seconds for me to see I was up against something that Reed would have been drooling over.

It was a seventies-era Chrysler that looked like a boat on wheels. I floored my BMW but the Chrysler started closing the gap. I bumped onto 394 proper and was surprised to see the Chrysler ease off the ramp perfectly, which was impressive considering it was a damned old car, maybe even from before the days of electric steering, and they were doing over 90 miles per hour.

"Shit," I said, realizing exactly who was behind me. "That's Garrett Breedlowe."

"Who?" Kat asked, sitting up in her seat.

Garrett Breedlowe had been a tatted-up gangsta-wannabe from Houston, Texas, who'd led a small gang of metas. There were three of them—Garrett, the ringleader, his sister Tasha Breedlowe Kern, who I had nicknamed "Crazyass," and Tasha's man, Peter Kern.

Peter Kern had been human while the Breedlowes were meta. When Reed and I had landed hard on them and whipped the Breedlowes, Peter hadn't gotten the news flash. He'd pulled a gun and damned near capped Reed in the back of the head.

I'd shot him right through the brain before he could do it.

This had happened months and months ago, before we left the government's employ, but I was guessing Tasha and Garrett hadn't forgiven or forgotten. I didn't recognize the Chrysler, but when I looked back I could see a front plate that identified it as a Minnesota-registered vehicle. "That's grand theft auto, I bet."

"You're worried about that right now?" Kat asked, betraying the first hint of her own worry.

"No, but it gives us a reason to call the cops on them," I said. "Dial 911 and give them our location, tell them some driver in a seventies Chrysler is weaving crazy all over the road." That was a lie. The Breedlowes were what Sienna called "Reflex types." Any action they saw performed, they could instantly absorb into their own muscle memory. Whichever of them was behind the wheel only needed to watch one NASCAR race and they'd be an expert driver instantly. Same thing with viewing a shooting competition; they'd be able to hit the target every time thereafter.

Kat pulled up her phone and dialed. I waited for her to start talking as the Chrysler closed the distance on me. I was pushing the BMW, pedal to floor along the straight stretch of 394, the soundproofing barriers on either side of the highway flying past. A building with Target's bullseye on its side shot into and out of view as the Chrysler continued to draw nearer and nearer.

"Hey, it's me," Kat said, and it took my brain a second to register that she had not dialed 911 as I had asked. "We've got trouble on 394—" I stared at her, flabbergasted, my attention off the roadway. I was about to ask why in hell she'd completely disregarded what I'd asked when there was a thump on my trunk.

I looked back in the rearview and saw feet standing on the back of my car. They were small feet, too, which told me I had picked up a spare passenger named Tasha Kern. I couldn't see her face because it was above the roofline, though not quite visible in the moonroof, but I knew she was back there, and Garrett was now brightlighting me from less than ten feet behind my trunk. If I stopped too suddenly, his big metal beast would plow right through the BMW, probably leaving nothing behind but a few pieces and a schmear of human gore where Kat and I had once been. "Dammit. That's Tasha."

"Ummm, this is bad," Kat said in a moment of classic understatement as she tried to look up through my moonroof.

"No duh shit," I said, and the roof started to squeal behind me. I didn't bother to look back, instead swerving slightly. The Chrysler blocked me instantly, forcing me in the other direction lest I inadvertently cause him to hit me with what the cops call the PIT maneuver. It's where they bump a car they're pursuing just beside the rear bumper and cause them to fishtail out. In my case, we were going fast enough that it was possible we'd flip.

"Ermagerd!" Kat screamed as I yanked the wheel in the opposite direction. "Why is he doing that? Isn't he worried about her falling?"

"They're Reflex types," I said, gripping the wheel so tight and tense I was afraid my shoulders were going to explode. "She could jump off at this speed and probably land in a roll so graceful she'd come out of it better than we would gliding to a stop in this car." That presented a real problem, I realized as Tasha Breedlowe Kern continued to peel the roof off my car. Garrett would try and keep us on the straight and narrow until she had a chance to get in and ... well, I wasn't sure what she was going to do once she got into the car, but I wasn't excited about fighting a reflex type in a vehicle doing over a hundred miles an hour on the freeway. I tried to slow down but Garrett was there, catching me under the back bumper and pushing with his muscle machine. I watched the speedometer climb even though my foot was off it.

"Maybe ... turn us over?" Kat asked, staring at me wide-eyed.

"Voluntarily?" I asked, feeling sick to my stomach. I looked back and saw that Tasha had ripped off about six inches of my roof at the rear. She kicked the glass a couple times and it burst, shattering into pebbled shards. "Or we could wait for the cavalry, right?" She stared at me blankly. "You did just call Sienna, didn't you?"

"Oh!" Kat started, eyes going wide. "No. I called my publicist. I should totally call Sienna!" and she went back to her phone, dialing frantically and then holding it up to her ear as the rear of the roof ripped another few inches. "Hmm," Kat said, "I got her voicemail ... Hey, it's Kat, we're under attack on 394 outside—well, we're passing the exit for highway 100 and—"

"OH SHIT!" I shouted as Tasha ripped the roof off a whole 'nother foot. We were not going to be able to wait for Sienna before solving this problem. My mind was racing; flipping the car was an unreasonable suggestion, but we were in an unreasonable position. The thing about that was after we flipped the car, Garrett would be fine, and would stop and probably kill us before we recovered from whatever damage we suffered from crashing in excess of a hundred miles an hour. And that was if Tasha didn't survive and beat him to it. She was an imaginative little hussy, as my mom would say, and the things she'd done to torment some of her victims made me shiver more than the cold air flowing in through the soon-to-be-convertible roof.

"Yeah, this is bad," Kat said mildly and looked around. "No trees between us and the freeway walls, either." She shrugged. "I got nothing."

"Yeah, and here I am in the middle of …" I almost slapped myself in the head. "… in the middle of a freeway of asphalt which is made of rock and stone and tar." I threw a nasty glance back to see Tasha's bare midriff, which was framed by low rise shorts and a high-rise blouse. Girl knew she was rocking that body.

I reached out ahead of us, way out of ahead of us so I'd have time to work before we passed the spot I was using my powers on. I broke a pothole-sized chunk out of the pavement and it rose out of the road in front of us. I shot it toward us, sending it at Tasha, hoping she might just be too focused on ripping the roof off my car to see it coming.

"You just made a huge pothole in the middle of the interstate!" Kat shouted.

"It's Minnesota, no one's going to notice," I said, still waiting to see if it hit home.

No such luck. With a shout of surprise, Tasha leapt off my car as the pavement chunk came shooting past like an asteroid. I didn't get to see her leap—the roof was in the way—but I was pretty sure it would have been enough to score a gold medal in the Olympics. Then she came down and stuck the landing, and the judges would have been all 10.0.

"Dammit," I muttered. I was going to have to get a little more creative than one chunk of pavement. I reached out ahead again, this time pulling from the lanes on either side of us. I'd done similar things before; I called it my pavement shotgun, because I'd rip the gravel components out of the tar and it'd blow wide like buckshot and fill my opponents with a lot of little pieces of rock. I was planning a big blast with this one, though, because I wanted to pepper the hell out of Tasha and also get Garrett off my ass at the same time.

I could touch the rock buried in the asphalt, reaching out with my mind. It was right there, a thousand little pieces on either side. I waited until we drew close, night air still whipping in the car around me, and then I pulled my hand down like I was pumping my fist. I didn't need to do it, but it felt right.

A few stray pebbles burst the front windows around us and Kat screamed. I heard and felt Tasha leap again, grunting as she did so, the suspension bouncing as she left my car. The sound of shattering glass came from behind us, too, and I watched Garrett's windshield and side windows shatter under the gravel buckshot burst. His head disappeared as he ducked down, and I suspected I'd missed the slippery little shit. The Chrysler kept right on our tail, pushing us forward, and Tasha landed on the trunk again, bouncing us slightly and reminding me that, once more, I'd failed to extract us from this crapstorm.

"Uhhh … what now?" Kat asked, a trickle of blood running out of her hairline. One of the stray pebbles must have gotten her, but she didn't seem to care, and it looked pretty superficial.

"One last play," I said, reaching down deep. I'd tried the easy way with one pothole. I'd tried the middle road by trying to shotgun these a-holes off my tail. None of that had worked, and I was through being Mr. Nice Guy.

I reached out ahead of me once more, as the roof tore off at the midpoint. Tasha could have probably squeezed in if she'd wanted to. I figured she was waiting to see if we were armed and going to shoot at her, and not for the first time in my life, I was wishing I carried a gun all the time like Sienna. I hadn't been carrying since we'd left government service— the University of Minnesota was pretty clear where they stood when it came to students carrying guns on campus— but everywhere else was fair game, and this was an oversight I meant to rectify as soon as we got back from California. I couldn't afford to go around unarmed anymore, not in my line of work.

"It'd be nice to put a few rounds in her legs right now," I muttered to myself as I concentrated.

"Oh!" Kat said, and pulled a pistol out of her handbag. She looked over her shoulder and took careful aim, then shot Tasha once in each knee.

"Aieeeeee!" Tasha screamed. She shuddered, the pain halting her progress at ripping off the roof of the car. Her head was still hidden by the roof, or I would have told Kat to just bust one in her dome and be done with this.

"Yeah," I said, irritated that Kat hadn't done that five minutes ago. "Like that." I put aside recrimination and thought real hard about what I was gonna do, because it was going to take all my focus to pull this one off.

I dug at a section of pavement in front of us, put all my thought into it. This wasn't no small pothole, and it wasn't a carwash blast of gravel, either. Stopping these two was going to be a full tilt boogie, and I was about to become the road warrior of freeway combat.

"Here we go," I muttered, and ripped the loose the first chunk of road, creating another pothole and hurling it at Tasha. She gasped and leapt once more as it soared, yelling as blood spattered on the trunk when she jumped. The asphalt chunk smacked against the peeled-up roof of the car as it shot past then ricocheted up and spun off as I let it leave my control. I was done with it anyway, and on to the second part of my evil genius plan.

Tasha was a badass, no doubt, with mad skills of gymnastics that would allow her to control her body in the middle of her leap. She could twist left and right, and probably dodge bullets in mid-air.

But bullets were small, and Tasha couldn't fly; she could just twist when she was airborne. Just like Garrett could drive—drive like a mofo, in fact—but he wasn't invincible in that car, because the Chrysler still had limits to its turn radius and acceleration. The Breedlowe siblings were still bound by the laws of physics, and that was their weakness.

I ripped up three lanes of pavement in front of us, leaving

a small hole in the middle, just big enough for a BMW to drive through. I brought all three lanes up in a ninety-degree angle, like a wall in front of us, and then tipped them toward each other as I drove through the little hole I'd left as my own personal escape route.

"AGHHHHH—" There was a *SPLAT!* as Tasha hit the roof of my impromptu tunnel at a hundred plus miles an hour. Even for a meta, that's terminal velocity, and I knew she wasn't rolling away from that shit. Zero point zero, lady; your vault was a fail.

I slammed my foot on the accelerator as we passed under the tunnel of safety. Making like that old Irish blessing, I had the rocky under-road rise up to greet my tires so I didn't rip my transmission out when we hit the massive gap left by the pavement I'd just torn up. I turned my eyes to the rearview again just in time to see Garrett Breedlowe with his mouth open in a scream that I could just barely hear as several tons of pavement crushed his Chrysler beneath it. The long hood of the car escaped, just barely, and the engine burst out of the grill and rolled along the dirt under-road behind us for a hundred yards.

I guided the BMW back onto solid pavement and then let out a breath of relief. Ripping up that much concrete would have been impossible a year ago, but Sienna had been pushing us all to the limits of our powers. Every day it seemed like she was throwing something new at us, and she'd even had the agency buy a disused rock quarry where I was training.

"It's all paying off," I whispered, reaching up to mop my brow. My face was wet, and for a second I worried it was blood. It wasn't, though. I was sweating like it was midsummer in Atlanta from the exertion, and I looked back again to see my handiwork.

Kat was looking, too. "I guess 394 West is going to be shut down for a while."

"Like anyone's gonna notice another road closure in this town," I said, wiping away the sweat as I sped up. I'd feel a lot safer once we were at the airport, with Sienna close at hand. Girl knew how to fight, and I counted myself lucky she was teaching me all the stuff she was. Kat looked at me funny. I just kept my eyes on the road and smiled. "Like they say, Minnesota's only got two seasons—winter and road construction." She snorted a little bit and we kept on, rushing like mad to get our asses out of that town before anything else bad happened.

17.

Sienna

I waited on the tarmac at the Eden Prairie airport with J.J. and Abigail, the two of them snuggling ridiculously behind me. I cast the occasional glance back, trying not to look bitter when I did. She was leaning against him, his hand patting her back, her head nestled beneath the crook of his chin, and I felt … sorry for myself, actually. A trickle of regret coursed through me and settled in my stomach. I suddenly wished I hadn't sent my boyfriend away.

"The plane's fueled and ready to leave," Ariadne announced, typically businesslike, her heels clipping briskly along against the tarmac. She was wearing one of her skirts with a blouse and a business jacket, like she was ready for a day of work, roller suitcase trailing along behind her and clicking on the seams of the pavement. She set it upright, the telescoping handle like a dual flagpole, and then set her heavy, expensive leather handbag on top of it. "Now we're just waiting on the others."

"Yeah," I said, tension infusing me. I could probably have used a massage—which was true almost day of my life. Unfortunately, it's hard to get a massage when your skin kills people. Not impossible, but logistically difficult.

An ambulance came rolling up, and the back doors sprang open to reveal Dr. Perugini, arguing with another paramedic. "You put in an IV like you are stabbing him with a knife! Has no one taught you to do this thing?"

"Ma'am—" the paramedic started.

"Doctor!" Perugini corrected.

"Glad you made it," I said, trying to head off what looked like an argument. Reed's eyes were now open, and he was watching the back-and-forth between Perugini and the paramedic warily, like he was expecting things to blow up any moment. The swelling on his face was much reduced already, which made it easier for me to take a breath of relief. "And you're awake, big brother."

"I already feel at least a hundred percent better," Reed said weakly.

"That is the morphine," Perugini said.

"Oh," Reed said, looking around. "Well, okay, then." He looked at me. "How are you doing?"

"I'm just dandy," I said. "Might go out dancing later, if you all will clear out in an expedient fashion."

A squeal of tires prompted me to spin around. Augustus's BMW came surging around the corner of a hangar, its roof torn off and looking like a metal leaf, crumpled and sticking upright. It was barely holding to the front of the car, and I could see him behind the steering wheel with Kat next to him as he pulled to a stop beside us. "What the hell happened to you?" I asked as he popped out, a sheen of flop sweat visible on his forehead.

"Check your messages," Augustus said, opening the backseat and pulling out a bag. He dusted off a hundred beads of safety glass from it as he extracted it, and I realized his back window was completely missing. "Short answer is we ran into the Breedlowe and Kern connection in Golden Valley."

"I never liked those two," Reed said, voice weak and woozy.

"You'll like them better now, though," Kat said, "in their new and improved pancake form."

I stared at her with brow furrowed, trying to puzzle out what she'd just said. "Huh?"

"I mashed them," Augustus said tightly. "You'll hear all about it on the news tomorrow, probably."

"Did you leave a massive crime scene behind?" I asked.

"It was self-defense," Kat said. "Honest."

"Awww, man," I said, putting a hand up to my forehead and squeezing the tight scalp just above my hairline. "Scott's totally going to blame this on me."

"Scott?" Reed asked. "What?"

"He's in town," I said, shaking my head. "I saw him at your house after you left."

"I don't remember leaving," Reed said, speaking to the sky above us. "When did I leave?"

"Perhaps less morphine," Perugini decided.

"Whatever, you're all here," I said, shaking off the bad mojo that seemed to be thick in the air around me this last day. "Let's get you loaded up and outta this state, okay?"

"Private plane, here we come," J.J. said, relinquishing Abigail. It was awkward. Not her—she extracted herself flawlessly. He kinda bumped around, the little geek, swinging his bag around and nearly taking her out at the knees. She deftly avoided it at the last second, and he said, "Oops. Sorry." She just smiled and started toward the plane, which had its stairs/door down and waiting for them. "Hey, Sienna?" J.J. gave me a look before he followed her. "I'll let you know what I find, okay?"

"Counting on you," I said, patting myself on the back for not commenting at all on his clumsiness. "Go get 'em, J.J."

"I will," J.J. said, "if they have wifi on the flight. Otherwise, you'll hear from me when we're in Cali." And he disappeared up into the private plane with his girlfriend—which I guess goes to show you that miracles can happen after all.

"You're flying escort for a while, right?" Augustus asked, stopping about a foot from me.

"All the way across South Dakota," I said with a nod. "Wyoming hasn't cleared me, so …"

"We'll be all right from there." He leaned in and gave me a hug with one arm, squeezing me tight. "You gonna be all right?"

"As long as you all are safe, I'll be fine," I said. I was lying, but not much.

"I rate that as mostly true," Kat said. I saw she was bleeding from a scalp lac, and the dark liquid had left a trail down her otherwise flawless face. "Sienna can handle herself." She leaned in as Augustus stepped back and gave me a very light, very European kiss to each cheek. "Mwah, mwah. Take care, all right?" And she strolled toward the plane and up the stairs, not once tripping on her damned high heels.

"We'll keep an eye on Reed," Augustus said, and I could tell he was making me a promise.

"Keep an eye on yourself, too," I said. "PERSEC, remember?"

"I remember everything you teach me," he said with a nod, then slung his bag over his shoulder. "And, uh … you were right about the gun thing. We'll talk about getting me a permit when I get back, awright?"

That one came as a surprise. "Sure thing," I said, and he headed off.

"I notice you're not saying goodbye," Ariadne said, rolling her luggage behind her. "I don't know if I should read that as confidence or you trying to keep us from worrying."

"I'm pretty sure I'll be fine," I said, "but it's not like any of us know our expiration date. And I do have a couple of very dangerous assassins supposedly after me."

She looked at me very evenly, betraying nothing. "Are you going to 'smoke them out,' as I think you'd call it?"

"I'm gonna smoke 'em, all right," I said. "Take ca—"

Kiss her goodbye for me, Eve said, bursting into my thoughts unasked.

"Ugh, no," I said, drawing up short. "Boundaries."

Ariadne blinked at me as she pulled away. "… What?"

Do it, Eve said.

"Compromise," I ground out through gritted teeth and leaned in to give Ariadne a hug that caught her completely off guard. Her eyes were wider than my ass as I broke from her. "That … was mostly not me."

She stiffened, bristling slightly. "I …" She stood there, composing herself. "Very well," she said finally, and walked off with her suitcase clattering behind her, her head down. She didn't look back.

"You really do have a way with people," Reed said as Perugini and the paramedic rolled him up to me.

"I went to the Sierra Nealon Homeschool of Charm," I said, watching Ariadne wobble a little in her heels. That wasn't normal. "What do you expect?"

"What I get, mostly," Reed said. He grabbed my hand. His was cold and clammy. "Where's Hampton?"

"I sent him away."

"Sienna," he groaned, sounding very disappointed in me. "Why?"

"Because it's hard times, Reed," I said. "On a normal day, we're the hunters. Today, we're prey to some of the most dangerous people on the planet. The natural order is flipped, and I don't want the rest of you to have to hold on while I turn it back over, so …"

"So you're gonna go it alone," he said. "Haven't you learned your lesson about that by now?"

"Again," I said, feeling like I was having to explain this once more because of the morphine, "any other day, we're a team. You guys are awesome. You're getting better all the time, and I'm proud of you. But this is the world turned on its ear, this is hell and high water rushing in, and we can't even tell which direction it's coming from." I kept a stiff upper lip. "I know you're all strong. That you all can fight. That none of you are weak.

"But you … are my weakness," I said. "If Cassidy is running this show, like she did last time … she knows that. She knows the way to hit Sienna is to hit you, Augustus, Ariadne, J.J.—"

"And me, of course," Perugini drawled with sarcasm.

"Of course," I said, looking at her with all sincerity. "If anything happened to you, Isabella—" she blinked at me using her first name, "—I'd go mad with rage. I'd kill whoever did it, and it would be bloody and slow."

She stared at me, eyes wide. "I … thank you?"

"It's her highest compliment, killing people in rage," Reed

said, patting her on the hand. He looked back at me, and his eyes were bleary and a little unfocused. "Do me a favor, though. This Hampton thing? Keep him on speed dial. The guy wants to help you."

"I'll think about it. But—"

"Dark and difficult times, I heard you," he said. "But sometimes ... you can use a hand during those times. And not just so you have another fist to beat your enemies to death with." He slapped my hand gently, clasping it for a full five seconds. "You're not invincible, Sienna, even without us standing around to give your enemies targets. You have feelings. You can get overwhelmed, I've seen it. Don't cut yourself off from everybody while you go do this thing, okay?"

I didn't know quite what to say. "I ..." I swallowed hard. "It's not like I can say, 'Please, just hold my hand,' when it comes to comfort ... you know?" I sniffed, doing that thing where I try and wall myself off from my emotions.

"Let him in, Sienna," Reed said softly. "Don't let Zack be your Vesper Lynd, okay?"

Zack bristled in my head. *He's calling me a* girl.

"Shut up, you're proving him right," I muttered under my breath, causing Reed to look around, as if trying to see who I was talking to. "I'll ... try," I said.

"If you really try," Reed said, as the paramedic started to wheel him away, "you'll succeed! It's not like this should be hard for someone who singlehandedly killed the most powerful man on the planet!" He tried to twist to keep speaking to me as they wheeled him off, but grimaced as he moved. "Okay, okay. Maybe not move like that just yet. Owwww."

I watched them go, Augustus standing at the bottom of the stairs, apparently to help bring Reed into the cabin. My phone started to buzz, and I answered it. "Oh, now you hear it ringing?" Augustus called back to me.

I waved him off. "Hello?"

"Sienna," Dr. Zollers said from the other end, and I could hear road noise whooshing in the background. "I got your message."

"And?"

"I'm on my way out of town now," he said. "I'll be in Iowa before sunup."

"My condolences."

He chuckled. "It's not that bad. I'll find somewhere to lay low."

"Destroy your phone as soon as we finish talking," I said. "Memorize my number, and don't call it except in an emergency."

"How will I know when it's safe to come back?"

I smiled. "You'll know."

"Oh, it's going to be one of those, is it? Big mess?" He sounded a little sad. "Take care, Sienna. Usually after those big messes, you're not exactly copacetic."

I knew what he meant. "I'll hold it together as best I can," I said. "Try to be a danger to others who deserve it rather than myself."

"You do that," he said. "I'll check in on you … the usual way … every now and again."

"See you in my dreams, doc."

"Go get them, Sienna."

I hung up and turned around just in time to see the door to the airplane closing. The engines were thrumming to life, and it started to taxi toward the runway. I took a long breath of cold autumn air as I stared out at the sky. I couldn't see a single star under the blanket of light pollution that the Twin Cities metro area gave off. My breath fogged as it came out. The plane started to head toward the runway, speeding up as it cornered. It paused, and then the engines throttled up; it surged ahead, zooming toward the end of the runway as I lifted off the ground. Its nose pulled up, and the wheels left the ground, and I accelerated after it.

In that plane was almost everyone in the world that I cared about, and the few who weren't in it were leaving Minneapolis-St. Paul. Giving me room to work. Giving me space to breathe, to stalk, to hunt.

To do what I did best.

The plane turned west, and I followed a few hundred yards back, eyes sweeping in front of me and behind. I'd watch them until I felt sure that they were clear of Cassidy's—or whoever was orchestrating this—clutches. Then it was going to be time for me to turn around and head home.

Time to go to work.

18.

I breezed into a diner on the west side of the cities a little after sunup, half frozen from my flight across South Dakota and shivering just a scosh. The hostess waved me up to the counter without bothering to ask if I wanted a table, because I came to this restaurant fairly often and I never wanted a table unless I was with someone. The place was somewhat crowded, TVs going where they hung behind the counter, stupid news networks doing their usual "Feed the audience scary bullshit until they become too paralyzed to change the channel" routine. In this case it was footage of all the metas being released from the Cube, apparently taken yesterday. Maybe they meant it to seem like *Suicide Squad*, but it looked more like dark SUVs rolling past the cameras with only brief glimpses of some of the faces of my greatest hits barely visible in the tinted windows.

"What'll you have, hun?" Karen was manning the counter. I knew her from coming in before. She was of the old school of waitresses, probably nearing fifty, and had clearly been doing this for a long while. She knew me, and probably knew who I was, though she was too Minnesota Nice to comment on it. She just treated me like any other customer, and I kept coming back because of it.

"Coffee," I said, and she had an empty cup in front of me almost instantly. "A world of coffee."

"Preference on kind?" she asked.

"I honestly don't care," I said, "as long as it's coffee. It can be unfair trade, sprayed with every toxic chemical known to

102

man, genetically engineered from sawdust and sarin gas, harvested by child slave labor, and brewed in the skins of the innocent, so long as it's not decaf."

She took this in with bleak amusement. "I don't think we have any of that."

"Just as well," I said as she tipped her carafe to fill up my mug with a steaming helping of black coffee, "I probably don't need the guilt that would come with it."

"Rough night?" She kept her eyes on the coffee as she poured.

"I haven't slept in a couple days," I said. "Just got back into town yesterday afternoon, in time to get some shit news. To celebrate that, I did some drinking, then I got in a fight. Then I had to say goodbye to … some people." I picked up the cup and burned my tongue as I poured it down. *Wolfe,* I commanded, and my tongue and esophagus felt better instantly. "Anyway … it's been a day."

"Sounds like," Karen said, darting a look at the TV over her shoulder. "You see this?"

"Hard to miss," I said with a fair dose of irony.

"Can't believe they're just lettin' 'em go," she said, close to mutinous. "World's gone crazy. Hardened criminals. Why don't they just open the gates at Stillwater Prison, too, let everybody out?"

"Might be less dangerous," I agreed, downing another gulp of coffee.

"You see what happened out there this morning?" She waved a hand toward 394, which was about a hundred yards out the front door. "Cops came in this morning, said they identified two bodies. Two of the prisoners that got out yesterday." I wondered about then if she maybe didn't know who I was, or if she was just really slick and fishing for info. "Figure they were chasing somebody. Somebody with powers, and that somebody got the better of them."

"You don't say."

"I guess there were a couple other incidents already, too," Karen went on, leaning an elbow on the counter and looking up at the TV. "Attacks, they said. They shoulda just kept these assholes locked up forever." She turned around on me, looking aghast. "Not that I'm against metas or anything. My brother-in-law's sister is one, and she's the sweetest thing, but …" She shuddered and shook her head. "These ones seem pretty damned irredeemable. Doesn't seem right to let 'em loose after what some of them have done."

"I can't disagree," I said, holding in the rest of my thoughts.

"You know what you want?" Karen asked, and I thought about it for a second. "The usual?"

"Sure, let's make it easy," I agreed. My brain was flatlined anyway, tired after all the running and fighting and bad news and crushing disappointment of these last couple days. Also, jet lag. And non-jet lag.

"Coming right up," and she wrote out my usual order on a little slip. It was a fried egg sandwich with oozy yolk, tomato, mayo and avocado on thick slabs of sourdough toast with a side of lovely fried potatoes. I drooled as I watched her slap the order under the pass to the kitchen and someone breezed by to collect it.

I sat there, lost in thought, my brain slowed to a crawl by fatigue as I tried to catalog everyone who had reared their ugly heads at us in the last day. Lorenzo Benedetti and the four Clarys were in custody, Garrett Breedlowe, Tasha Breedlowe Kern, and Fintan O'Niall—none whom I knew well—were all dead, removed from the board by my friends.

That left, by my reckoning, a shit ton of bad guys either probably stalking me or else out of sight, status undetermined. For all I knew, Timothy Logan had already banded his four assholes back together and decided to switch their objective from robbing a lab in Oregon to plastering my brains all over the sidewalk as revenge for ruining their plans. It was a long shot, but I couldn't rule it out. Plus, if Thunder Hayes and his cronies were to be believed, Rosanna Borosky and Michael Shafer (a.k.a., Iron Tooth) were definitely intent on killing me. With Cassidy out there, and Eric Simmons possibly still with her, and a goodly number of other associated assholes just floating in the wind, I wasn't too happy about where I was standing in all this. Not that I objected to being surrounded, but I felt both surrounded and blind. Not a great combo, especially for someone as powerful as I was, because lashing out blindly in all directions meant you might just hit someone you didn't mean to. In a city of 3.5 million people, that was a lot of collateral damage I needed to avoid.

"You watching this?" Karen asked as she came back by. I stirred and realized she was talking about the news. A morning show had replaced the taped feeds of the prisoner release, and the volume tab was sliding up. I realized Karen had the remote in her hand, and suddenly my meta hearing kicked in to deafening proportions as I focused in on the TV and she kept turning it up.

"—new allegations this morning," the hostess was saying, staring right into the camera with that grave concern mingled with morning pep, "of prisoner abuse in the metahuman containment facility in Minneapolis as well as wrongful imprisonment claims. I have with me as my guest Owen Traverton." The camera panned out to show the hostess sitting on the couch next to a skinny white guy who looked like he'd been whacked with a rolled-up newspaper a few too many times. In fact, he hadn't been hit with one nearly enough, in my opinion. "Owen has spent the last eight months incarcerated in what is colloquially known as 'The Cube.' Good to have you here with us, Owen."

Owen twitched. "It's good to be here. It's actually good to be anywhere now that I'm out of that …" He shuddered, leaving his cruel torment to our imaginations.

"That son of a bitch," I said, not even bothering to hold it under my breath.

"You know him?" Karen asked, not even giving me a glance, riveted by the scene unfolding before us.

"Thought I did," I said. "He's a dog." I meant that mostly literally; Owen Traverton was an animal shapechanger who had posed as my dog for several months in order to spy on me for Cassidy and the Clary family.

"—and so you were—you feel—wrongfully incarcerated?" the hostess asked, full of sympathy for poor, poor abused Owen. I wished he were right in front of me so I could have whapped with something harder than a newspaper, like my fist. I wasn't at all in favor of animal abuse, but he could have turned into dog form, stared at me with sad dog eyes, and I still would have smashed his face in.

"They had no reason to hold me," Owen said, poor puppy dog eyes looking oh-so-beleaguered. "Sienna Nealon threw me in there before she quit working for the government. The guards said when they released me that they didn't even have a reason recorded on my file." He shook, ever so slightly. "She left the government months ago, and no one ever even asked me why I was in there. They had no idea."

"That's appalling," the hostess said, and her mouth open to convey shock and disbelief. "So you're saying they had no cause to hold you?"

"That's what the guards told me when they let me out," he said. "That's what my lawyer said, too, when he got a chance to look at the file. If not for this court decision, they might have kept me imprisoned there … forever." He poured it on, like a terrible actor, hamming it up for the camera. I restrained myself from throwing my silverware, which was the only thing within easy reach, at the TV. It wasn't easy.

"Yeah, I just bet," Karen scoffed, turning the volume back down. "You just happened to get thrown in jail for no reason. None at all." She shook her head and turned back to me.

"I hope other people see it the way you do," I said, taking another long drink of my coffee.

Something jangled, loud enough to get my attention, and I swept the restaurant with my eyes before realizing it was the TV again, and one of those "BREAKING NEWS" alert noises had just played, interrupting the sad-sack-fest with Owen the dirty dog. The screen switched back to a studio with a newscaster behind the desk, this time one of those distinguished gentlemen with a voice you could trust. Or so you were meant to believe.

"We interrupt this broadcast to bring you breaking news," he said, looking right into the screen and speaking, leaning heavy on his solemn credibility. "Two sources within the Harmon administration have confirmed for us this morning something that's been long rumored—" A picture flashed up in the corner of the screen. A picture of me. "—That in the closing days of Sienna Nealon's war on Sovereign, she received a presidential pardon for several murders she'd committed before that fight's conclusion. We go live to Robin Judd in Minneapolis, who has more—"

Karen didn't look at me, didn't take her eyes off the screen. "Well, hun," she said, shaking her head, "I guess today's not going to be any better for you than the last one." And she filled my cup again.

19.

After breakfast, I headed to the office, circling the area around it a few times. It was hardly a conclusive sweep, but I didn't see any obvious evidence that it was being watched—no unattended cars I didn't recognize, no mysterious silhouettes in the windows in surrounding buildings. It was just after sunup, and everything seemed to be as it was supposed to be, at least in the area surrounding my office.

Unfortunately, one of the things that was apparently now normal was the presence of Thunder Hayes, Bronson McCartney and Louis Terry at the ice cream parlor next door, which wasn't even open yet. I came down for a landing just out from the overhang where the three of them were all chortling at some joke, prompting them all to gawk at me.

"Morning, boys," I said, pretty skint on amusement.

"Heyyyy," Hayes said, lifting a red Solo cup to me in salute. "Heard you got problems, Nealon."

"Oh, yeah?" I watched him and his cronies carefully. They didn't seem to be making any overtly threatening moves, but that was hardly conclusive with this rabble. "How'd you hear that?"

"With my ears," Hayes said, and McCartney and Terry burst out laughing. I let them have their moment, and as Hayes started to settle down, he said, "It was on the TV at the diner down the road." He looked faux-earnest for a second. "Murder? Really?"

"You seem surprised," I said. "As though you didn't watch me empty Crow Vincent's head right in front of you."

Hayes froze, ruddy skin flushing red. "I do recall that. That was damned vicious."

"He was asking for it," I said lightly, looking them all over. "Kinda like you, right now."

"Ohh, scary," McCartney said, the big lug. "You gonna attack us?"

"You know how I know you're stupid, McCartney?" I asked, sidling up to him and putting my foot right on the bench next to him. I leaned forward, and what with me being so short and him being so tall, I had to look up to smile sweetly in his eyes. "Because you know who I am, you know at least a little of what I'm capable of, what I've done to you and to others—when I was restrained, which I'm fast approaching not being—and you're still here taunting me."

"Maybe we're just counting on the better angels of your nature to spare us poor, innocent souls who haven't done anything wrong," Hayes said with a sneer.

"I wouldn't count, if I were you," I said. "You're not smart enough to do it properly."

"Yeouch," Terry said. "Hurtful words."

"That's the least hurtful thing I've got at my disposal," I said, pulling my foot off the bench and turning to head to my office. I froze; there was shattered glass all across the concrete in front of the door.

"Oh, yeah," Hayes said, following my gaze. "Forgot to tell you about that."

"You broke into my office?" I felt the heat rising.

"Wasn't us, honest," Hayes said. "You should call the cops, I'll swear a statement. 'It was a wild raccoon, officer! Ain't never seen nothing like it!'" McCartney and Terry were guffawing again, and I resisted the urge to turn their heads inside out.

I turned around to see them sharing a good laugh. "Wild raccoon, huh?"

"Go check your security cameras," Hayes said, nodding, "you'll see it's true. I was here the whole time, watching. So was Terry. We heard an awful racket inside, and then the damned thing came busting out the front window. Skittered off down the street."

I looked right at McCartney, the animal shape-changer. "And you didn't see it?"

"I was in the bathroom down the road," McCartney said, sneering right at me with a defiance that sent my blood pressure soaring. "Didn't get back 'til it was over."

"What a magnificent coincidence," I whispered, my hand shaking at my side.

"Whoa, there," Hayes said, "careful. You wouldn't want to get in trouble with the law, trust me." His face stretched in a nasty smile. "I assure you that their accommodations for meta lawbreakers are anything but first class."

"Well, as you've just proven, Hayes," I said, probably sounding a little choked, "you really need a witness in order to prove wrongdoing these days." My lip twitched at the end, and I could feel interest rise in my head as Wolfe and Bjorn practically started panting.

"I think we might have a few," Hayes said coolly as tires squealed behind me.

I spun in time to see a news van coming down the street. It was probably the first of many that would be coming, and I cursed myself for not vaporizing these three earlier. It wasn't going to be too long before I found myself under siege here, a hundred cameras watching my every move.

"Buh bye!" Terry said, making a little wave with his fingers.

"See you later!" Hayes called after me as I stalked off toward my broken door. The front window was shattered, too.

"I should think so," I said, casting them a nasty smile that erased Hayes's, at least. I dodged into my office through the broken front door, out of sight of those three and trying to decide my next move.

20.

I kept the reporters outside my broken windows with threats of arrests for trespassing, the only non-violent means I had at my disposal. They filmed and snapped their pictures from outside the office, every word, every sound audible to me through the broken windows of the office. McCartney had busted them all, that crotchstain, and it left nothing but open air between me and my newfound stalkers in the press.

I tried to tune out their broadcasts from where I was sitting in a back conference room in the interior of the building, watching the stupid news with the sound muted. I didn't want the vultures to know I was watching them as they were watching me, but it gave me a pretty good view of my front door, side of the building, and even the rear entrance, which was useful since McCartney had also trashed the security cameras while in feral raccoon mode. I'd watched the footage up to that point, and he had indeed done it as a raccoon.

The reporters started yelling questions at someone outside, and I heard glass crunching underfoot as an unknown person brushed aside the front door blinds and stepped into the office's waiting area.

"Unless you want to get arrested for trespassing," I yelled for the thousandth time in the last two hours, "get the hell out!"

"I need to hire you," a quiet voice came back to me. A familiar voice which immediately put me on edge. Soft footsteps worked their way down the hall, and I drew

Shadow, holding the barrel up in anticipation as Timothy Logan's head came slowly around the corner.

He took in the gun pointed at his head, seemed to calculate the odds on it blowing his head off, and then eased his hands out where I could see them. "I'm unarmed, and I'm not looking for a fight."

"As though I give a shit about any of that." I kept the gun pointed at him, my stomach roiling in disgust. "Get lost."

"There's something going on here that you need to know about," he said, keeping his hands up.

I stared at him. "I can't even stand to look at you right now," I said, putting the blinding disgust I was feeling into my statement.

"I … I get that—" he said.

"I doubt it."

"But don't let your wounded pride get in the way of the bigger things going on here," he said. "I didn't just take that job at the lab because I needed the money."

"So you do pro bono criminal work?"

"No," he said, "but I did it because there is something going on at Palleton Labs that isn't right."

"Yeah," I said, "a bunch of metahumans broke in the other day. They got away with it, though."

"I'm not going to get away with it," he said, voice cracking.

"You're looking free as a bird to me," I said airily. I still had my finger on the trigger.

"Do you even want to hear what I've got to say?" He was looking at me with puppy dog eyes. Owen Traverton eyes, that was how I thought of them, as just another betrayal, and I resisted the temptation to spit right in his face.

"Nope."

I watched as his face fell. I didn't know what he'd had planned in coming here, but I could smell the disappointment. He even looked a little wounded, which made sense, because everything I'd said to him since he'd walked in had been exactly the sort of shit my mother used to badger me with when I disappointed her in some way. I'd learned well how to hurt people when I wanted to drive them away, and I wanted Timothy Logan to go find a fire and die in it, preferably while screaming loudly.

He turned around to leave, and let his hands slowly drop to his side, apparently convinced I wouldn't shoot him in the back. He was probably right, most days. Today, though, I thought about it. "You might regret this," he said.

"There are many things I regret in life," I said with great conviction. "Not ever really meeting my father. Agreeing to an interview with Gail Roth. That not-brief-enough period of time when I thought I could pull off twerking. But this?" I waved Shadow's barrel, careful to keep it aimed at his upper body. "This isn't even going to make the list below 'Having that extra margarita last night after beating the ass off the Clarys.'" I stood, and pulled Shadow's hammer back, letting that ominous click fill the air. "Don't ever let me see you again, Timothy, or I will shoot you in the back, front, or whatever piece of you that gets presented to me."

He didn't look back. "You won't ever see me again." And he walked out, leaving me to puzzle out what exactly he meant by that bit of ominousness.

21.

I had to unmute the TV when the words, "President Harmon holds press conference on Nealon pardon," appeared at the bottom of the screen in bold letters, which irritated the hell out of me. I turned the volume way, way down, and even that wasn't enough to mask the sound of Thunder Hayes doing his eighteen thousandth interview of the morning. He was not a quiet man, and I'd been fortunate enough to be able to listen, just-before-live, as he ran me down on every single network presently holding court in my parking lot.

Oddly enough, not one of the so-called journalists thought to ask what seemed to me a very basic question: *Gee, Mr. Hayes, why are you outside Ms. Nealon's office?* Apparently they didn't think it was at all unusual for newly released convicts to just hang around outside their arresting officer's place of business. Probably assumed they genuinely were here for the ice cream.

The network I was watching cut away from rerunning their interview with Thunder Hayes for the eighth time in the last half hour to show the empty podium of the White House press room. It was a good aesthetic choice, I thought, given that Thunder Hayes looked only marginally less attractive than a pig's ass but twice as hairy.

"We're waiting now for President Harmon's statement on the recent revelations involving Sienna Nealon's past," one of the offscreen commentating jackasses said breathlessly, as if that explained why they were wasting precious airtime on an empty podium, photogenic as that podium might have been when compared to their last interview subject. "He's expected to make a statement shortly." For this live shot of a podium they were passing on a commercial break in which they could sell me pads to deal with the incontinence caused by waiting to see what the president was going to say about me.

I waited with bated breath, wondering if I should risk sneaking into Ariadne's office to hit the bottle of brandy she kept hidden there. Downside: I might get seen by the reporters outside, because McCartney had ripped down the blinds in that room. Plus side: I might have liquor to endure whatever crap Harmon was about to say vis-à-vis me, provided McCartney hadn't destroyed the bottle. I gave it fifty/fifty whether Harmon was going to defend his decision to issue me a pardon or just toss me under the Acela, as one does when in Washington. (Because tossing one under the bus is just so last year.)

My phone buzzed, causing me to just about lose bladder control again. I'd been holding it in all morning because I didn't want to leave the interior room for fear that the press would interrupt the shot of the empty podium or a gripping rerun of the umpteenth Thunder Hayes interview to show me walking down a hallway. *Sienna Nealon walks down hallway!* the chyrons would declare, as though this were VERY IMPORTANT NEWS, critical to the well-being of every citizen of the world.

Did I mention that I hate twenty-four hour news stations? I feel I should mention that, again and again.

I scooped up the phone and unlocked it to find a text message from Veronika: *All arrived safely. I've arranged the safehouse, and all protectionary measures are in place. Augustus will call you to verify.*

The phone rang, and I answered it without checking the caller ID, something I never do. "Yes?" I whispered. Clearly the fear of being watched was making me crack up; answering the phone without checking on it, whispering in my own open-air offices ... this was not the behavior one would expect from Sienna Nealon, dammit.

"We made it," Augustus said.

"You sure?" I muttered, peering at the door to the hall as though a plethora of reporters armed with microphones and cameras were going to come bursting in any second. "You're not being forced to read a canned statement by someone with a gun at your head, are you?"

"Why would I—don't you think they'd want you to know they had us, if that were the case?" Augustus asked, poking his damned logic holes in my paranoid theory. "And why are you whispering?"

"Thunder Hayes and his crew of miscreants destroyed our offices last night."

"What?"

"Well, it was actually Bronson McCartney, in the form of a raccoon, but—"

"WHAT?!"

"Never mind," I said. "Anyway, we have no windows, and a murder of reporters is perched outside—"

"Wait, are you pluralizing reporters as—"

"A murder, yes, keep up. Anyway, they're outside, and I'm afraid they'll use long range microphones to listen in on our conversation."

There was a brief pause. "You know, about half the time I think your obsession with security is just crazy paranoia letting itself run loose."

"And the other half of the time?"

"I'm wishing I had a gun to blast the crazies that are legit after my black ass." He took a deep breath. "What's the move?"

"Your move is to stay hunkered down," I said. "This safehouse Veronika set up … is it really safe?"

He waited a moment before replying, and I could tell he was trying to decide whether to humor me or perhaps bust my ass. "It's got good lines of sight, your boy Phinneus is sitting about a half mile out keeping watch, and speedy Colin is doing loops with occasional breaks to lecture us all on sustainability. I'm thinking about setting up a glass trap for him again—"

"Just take the lecture with a smile and let him protect

you," I said.

"You say that because you ain't had to listen to his shit. If I hear one more diatribe on the toxic pestilence we're feeding ourselves by being non-organic and non-vegan, I'mma—"

"Sit back and listen to another one, and realize that while annoying, he's a great perimeter guard," I said.

"Perimeter, shmeshmimeter, he's a twat."

I frowned. "That's a very British thing to say. Where did you even learn that?"

"Pffft, I'm all cultured now, got class and sophistication." He gave it a second to sink in. "Also, it was on Netflix."

"*Downton Abbey*?"

"*Hot Fuzz*, I think? Reed recommended it. *Downton*'s in my queue, but Taneshia wants to watch it with me."

"Best to wait, then. I'd hate to see you go out, especially in such an electrifying manner."

"Terrible pun." I could almost imagine him shaking his head, the silence growing between us, suddenly uncomfortable as a fall breeze rattled some of the hanging blinds in the other room.

I shuddered in the chill. "You should probably put Veronika on."

"What, you can't call her on her own cell phone? People getting lazy these days—"

"Yeah," I said, "including ones who won't just hand a stupid phone over to someone standing next to them."

"Veronika isn't standing next to me." He grunted and I heard him walking, and then J.J.'s voice in the background:

"… but because they sold the rights, it's not an MCU movie."

Then I heard Veronika. "But it said Marvel on it."

"Yes," J.J. said, "but—"

"Yo," Augustus said, "Sienna wants to talk to you."

"I don't really have anything for her," J.J.'s voice broke through. "Yet, I mean."

"Maybe if you weren't trying to explain the defining lines of the MCU to Veronika, you might," Reed's voice came through the phone.

"This is important stuff, okay?" J.J. said. "*Deadpool* is not

MCU canon, and people need to know that."

"But it has—" Veronika started.

"IT IS NOT MCU CANON!" J.J. shouted.

"Oookay," Veronika said, and suddenly she got a lot louder. "Yo, girl. All quiet on the west coast front."

"Hey," I said, "thanks for handling this."

"No thanks needed," she said, "because I saw your wire transfer, and it was all the gratitude I require."

"Good to know," I said, and an ugly thought raised its head. "Listen, if anyone ever tries to outbid me—"

"Whoa, whoa," Veronika said. "You know I don't sell out my clients for a higher bidder, so no need to worry about doing a Dinklage here."

"A Lannister always pays their debts!" J.J. shouted in the background.

"… whut?" I asked.

"You don't watch *Game of Thrones*?" Veronika sounded mildly scandalized.

"No, I watch it, I'm just trying to put that one together."

"Bron and Tyrion, their arrangement to—you know what? Never mind. Deal's a deal, that's the point."

"I feel a lot more relieved now that the person who fights for money has made clear that she can't be bought out for more money," Augustus said in the background.

"You're cute, honey," Veronika said. "Go get me a Lipton's Tea out of the pantry, will you?"

"The hell?" Augustus asked. "Does this look 1963 South Carolina to you? What the shit? You gonna go sit on the porch and admire your plantation afterward?"

"Oh, don't be so damned sensitive or you'll never be able to handle the nipple clamps later," Veronika said, and I could hear her moving. "To say nothing of the pegging."

"The *what*?!"

"Anyway," Veronika said, sounding like she was back to concentrating on me, "I think your friends are under the radar, because no one's even approached me yet."

"That could change any minute," I said, feeling a tinge of loneliness knowing that pretty much everyone I cared about was at least a state away, if not many, many more.

"I'll let you know if anyone does make an offer, just so you know the direction the trouble's coming from, but—and I know this is gonna sound funny, but cash is bond. Your peeps are safe with me."

That lonely feeling got deeper, all the way down to a hollow core inside, like someone was plucking a harp string that was vibrating through an empty cave within me. I pushed that feeling away, trying to summon up a forced smile as I quipped: "You keep your damned plasma-burning hands off my marshmallow treats."

Veronika just laughed, thankfully getting the joke. "Do what you gotta do, sweetie. And watch your back."

"I'll tr—" I blinked; President Gerry Harmon had appeared at the podium. "I gotta go."

"Seriously. Watch your back, because you know no one else is there to do it."

"I know," I said, and hung up just in time to see the President of the United States smile smugly, right at the camera, and somewhere in my gut, I knew that what he was about to say next was going to be really, really bad.

22.

"Ladies and gentleman of the press," Gerry Harmon said, in a voice dripping with smarminess, "thank you for coming." I looked at the clock; he was at least seven minutes late. Apparently he didn't really have a lot of respect for reporters or punctuality. "I'm going to give a brief statement, and I won't be taking questions afterward." He looked up, as though challenging one of them to say something. No one did, so he stared right into the camera and started talking. I couldn't tell if he was reading from a teleprompter or if he'd memorized his speech.

"Five years ago, the world watched as a secret hidden for ages came out in the most stunning way possible—there were people with powers living and working among us, hidden in our own society under the surface. They'd been with us since the days before civilization, their stories fading into the realm of myth, an active conspiracy working to keep them hidden from our sight. You all know this, of course," he said, clearly pandering to his audience. *Oh, you're soooooo smart.* I imagined it being said by Kat, and it made me twitch. *You know all this already, you bright boy, you!*

You are very unkind to my sister, Gavrikov said, *and she is so very helpful to you.*

"Not now, Aleksandr," I said wearily. "But ... you're right."

My admission shut his mouth, which was good, because I was missing Harmon's speech. "... in a battle for the very survival of our people, our way of life, I was told. Told by people I trusted—at the time." Harmon was dropping the smugness by a few dozen degrees. Now he seemed humble. "I believed the extraordinary threat Sovereign posed to America, to the world. I have never disclosed the source of this knowledge, but in the course of what I am about to reveal today, it becomes important that you understand the factors that led to the decisions made to laud Sienna Nealon for what she's done—"

"Here we go," I said, unsurprised. He was setting it up to toss me right under that Acela.

"—the information I received came from my opponent in the last election, Senator Robb Foreman of Tennessee," Harmon said, and there were gasps in the press room. I found my lips curled up in a sneer, eyes rolling. He'd just tossed some company down onto the tracks with me. "I trusted Senator Foreman, not realizing at the time that he was aligning me with Sienna Nealon, probably for his own purposes. Obviously, his scheme failed, though only thanks to the judicious nature of the electorate."

I buried my face in my hands at this. I didn't want to watch his expression any more as he did what he was about to do.

"Senator Foreman assured me of the good character of Ms. Nealon," Harmon went on, "and told me that in the course of her battle with Sovereign, she'd violated the law. It was not until later that the full extent of her wrongdoing came to light. Let me say this as clearly as possible—I did not know, when I signed Ms. Nealon's pardon, exactly what she had done. It was a blanket pardon designed to insulate her against any attempt by local or state prosecutors, driven by fear of metahumans, to prosecute her for actions taken to protect humanity from Sovereign. It was not supposed to protect her from murders she committed in cold blood."

I sank back in my chair and the breath seeped out of my lungs slowly. The President of the United States had just told the world I was a murderer.

"As you all know," Harmon said, "Ms. Nealon left government service earlier this year, and I have instructed the FBI task force in charge of policing metahumans to keep close watch on her since, fearing she might revert to type. There is obviously no shortage of documentation— YouTube videos, eye-witness accounts, press incidents— showing us that Ms. Nealon is perhaps not even close to the image of an idealized hero that I was sold by Senator Foreman. Indeed, the Cube prison in Minneapolis was her idea—"

"You sonofabitch," I said under my breath.

"—designed and constructed under her supervision, filled by her and her hand-selected team. When my administration responded to reports of Ms. Nealon's illicit activities and prisoner mistreatment by placing her Metahuman Threat Response and Policing Task Force under the umbrella of the FBI and the Department of Justice's closer oversight, it was then that Ms. Nealon resigned, presumably in order to avoid the stricter watch that this might bring on her. As you further know, now she works in a freelance capacity for some of the states on contract—"

"You bastard, you bastard, you—" I said, over and over. My heart was plummeting like I'd flown high and suddenly lost my powers, dropping back to earth without anything but the hard ground to stop me.

"—where we have documented reports of her assisting individuals like Gravity Gal who have clashed with lawful authorities," Harmon said. All this was delivered with greatest sincerity; he'd buried his smugness so deep I doubted I could have found it with a bulldozer. I would have liked to have tried, though. Digging into him with a bulldozer would have been really fun right about then. "There remains a pattern of behavior from Ms. Nealon that suggests that she has not changed. Looking back to the incident in Los Angeles early this year, I directed the FBI to reopen a case the LAPD had already closed. FBI Director Phillips will be holding a briefing later this week to sum up the findings in detail, but for now, suffice to say that while the burden of evidence has not been met in order to bring charges against Ms. Nealon for her actions, there is no doubt in any of our minds that she has acted improperly, unnecessarily violently, and without the best interests of the public at heart. She has betrayed the public trust, misrepresented herself to all of us, and is likely continuing her established pattern of criminal wrongdoing. To Ms. Nealon I would say this: we know who you are now, and we are watching. For too long, you have relied on the good nature of the American people. Ours is a willingness to believe in others ... in the goodness of others. We have overlooked, we have ignored, and we have extended every opportunity to you to be the hero we thought you were.

"Those days are over. From this day forth, should Ms. Nealon commit so much as a misdemeanor, I have instructed the Department of Justice to prosecute her with all the force of statute available. There will be no more murders at her hand, no more excuses why the most powerful woman on the planet cannot restrain herself in her dealings with others. We have offered her a low standard, and she has taken full advantage of it; now we will hold her—and in time, perhaps other metas with her abilities—to the highest standards. We declare, today, that we will no longer tolerate the chaos she brings to our cities, to our communities, to our country." He looked right into the camera. "It ends today. Thank you," he said to the reporters, and the bastards started applauding. He basked, for just a moment, and then he swept off, leaving an empty podium once more, and me in absolutely no doubt of where I stood.

There were people hunting me. Serious people. Stone-cold killers. They were going to try and put me in the ground, there was no doubt in my mind.

And now, if anything happened to any of them, the US government was going to try and arrest me and put me in jail for defending my own life. "Welcome to the new box," I whispered to myself, listening to the voices of a hundred reporters outside my office, chattering like the herd animals they were, all saying the same thing—that my days as a free woman were drawing to an end.

23.

My phone started ringing a few seconds after the press conference ended, keeping me from hurling my phone, the closest thing at hand, into the television. This time I looked at the caller ID, and when I saw it was Jonathan Chang, my lawyer, I answered immediately. "I don't mean to sound like a seventies song, but tell me something good."

"Errr, hello to you, too, Ms. Nealon," Chang said, in that calm, polite, even tone he regularly employed. Chang was the guy who had acted as the middleman lawyer between the person who had funded my operation here at this new agency, and he'd also been the one fighting my legal battles for me whenever they'd come up. Mostly they were trivial things, with one exception—the FAA, who had decided I was no longer fit to fly the friendly skies. "I'm afraid I don't have any good news for you at this point, though."

"Bummer," I said, understating it. "Because I don't know if you just caught that press conference, but—"

"I was apprised of its contents about an hour before the president went on air," Chang said, sounding a little clipped. "Ms. Nealon … I'm afraid my firm can no longer act as the go-between for your employer and yourself."

"What the hell?" I didn't even think before asking.

"This doesn't mean your employer is firing you, by any means," Chang went on, sounding like he was reading from several pre-sorted talking points. "On the contrary, we've contacted your employer to tender our resignation as the firm of record in the matter of your new agency—"

"Uh, why?" I asked, then kicked myself for asking. "Wait. The publicity? I thought you lawyers love publicity?"

"Our firm does not particularly enjoy being in this sort of limelight, no," Chang said, sounding vaguely affronted, like I'd called his mother a ho. "When we took this position as go-between—"

"Middleman. Middlemen? Middledudes," I decided.

"You were certainly no stranger to controversy," he went on, undeterred by my smartassery. "But obviously new information has come to light in that regard—"

"You mean the President of the United States calling me a murderer on national television?"

"He actually didn't," Chang said. "He was very careful in what he said."

"So you're leaving me because you can't construct a libel suit?"

"We're not leaving you, Ms. Nealon," Change said. "We never worked for you. We work for your employer, and have contacted him with our notice of resignation, effective immediately, in this capacity. We wish you both the best of luck, and if we hear from your employer that he, too, wishes to sever connection with you—"

"Kick a girl while she's down, huh?"

"Not many people want to actively associate with someone accused of what you stand accused of," Chang said patiently. "And in case it is not abundantly obvious to you, let me spell this out in my last act as your lawyer—"

"You just said you weren't my lawyer—"

"I advise you, but I don't work for you," Chang said.

"You can save it," I said. "I get it. They're all after me, and if I step out of line, they're going to throw not just the book at me, but probably every single copy of the *Encyclopedia Britannica* that remains sitting on the bookshelves of old people without internet right directly at me."

"Colorful," Chang said.

"But accurate, no?"

"Very likely," Chang said. "I also wanted to inform you that in addition to the letter we received from the Harmon Administration, we also received at updated notice from the

FAA this morning, delivered in concert—"

"Like a symphony orchestra? Or was it a pop concert?"

"—informing us that the FAA is asserting federal authority over your traverse of airspace," Chang went on, once again ignoring me, probably so he could get me off the phone faster. "They are contesting your state-based exemptions, but I need to warn you that in addition to these two letters, we also received another notice from Governor Shipley's office—"

"This just keeps getting better and better."

"—and she's revoked your flight privileges over Minnesota, effective immediately," Chang said, "once again, on the recommendation of the Harmon administration."

"I feel like you could have delivered all that shit news more economically," I said. "You kind of spread it out, then layered it, a round at a time, one atop the next. You should have just dumped it all out thusly: 'Everyone says you can't fly anymore—Minnesota, the FAA. Also, Harmon thinks you suck, we think you suck, and we don't even want to work within a hundred mile radius of you anymore, crazypants.' See? That took like five seconds." I waited to see if he would respond. "Anything else? Say it quickly if you've got something."

"I wish you the best of luck, Ms. Nealon," Chang said stiffly. "I will be in touch if your benefactor has any message he wishes to pass along, once we hear from him."

"Thanks a lot," I said without much in the way of conviction, then hung up on him and deleted his number from my phone. Petty, maybe, but I didn't answer unknown numbers, and if it was important he could leave a damned message in my mailbox. At least the press hadn't found my cell phone number yet, though I was sure they would soon.

I dropped my phone back on the table and leaned back in my seat. This had certainly been a morning for kicking my teeth in. Not only had my lawyers dropped me, leaving me without a conduit to my mysterious employer, but I'd been denounced as a murderer on national television by the commander in chief, and my office was wrecked thanks to a human-turned-raccoon who was sitting right outside, and just outside the reach of the increasingly short arm of the law.

"Well," I said to myself, because there wasn't anybody else left to talk to, "this sucks." And it damned sure did.

24.

Sitting behind a desk without anything to do may sound like a fun way to spend a day, but if idle hands were the devil's play things, an idle butt planted in a chair was probably worse, because I still had the idle hands, too. I did sneak in and search Ariadne's office for brandy, and unfortunately, McCartney, that shitlord extraordinaire, had broken it all over her carpet. I should have known by the smell, but apparently there wasn't much left when he broke it, because it was a fairly small puddle. I'd gotten Ariadne the bottle when we'd started here, which meant she'd gone through almost the whole thing in six months or so. At work.

Then again, at the rate my day was going, I would have gone through it by lunchtime, so maybe six months for a whole bottle wasn't terrible. Especially since she was working on financials and spreadsheets and managing fallout from the crap I did. That was probably worth a shot a day by itself.

I kept myself from sinking so low as to lick up the brandy from the carpet (mostly because it was now dry, and thus pointless and not at all intoxicating) and instead float-crawled on my belly back to the interior office where the news was muted, bottom of the screen scroll touting, "MAJOR REVELATIONS IN SIENNA NEALON CASE." Now I had a case, and it wasn't of something to drink.

I drummed my fingers on the table and stared at the ceiling. There wasn't any décor on the walls because McCartney had ripped it all off. I was just lucky he hadn't trashed the TV. Maybe he knew it would be the instrument of my misery and decided to let it survive. Or, more likely, he trashed the place in such a hurry that he just missed it.

I didn't have a lot to go with at this point. I was basically waiting around for people to attack me, and it seemed like they weren't eager to do that if they had to cut through a press scrum to do so. Probably something about witnesses. Or maybe I was just paranoid for realsies, and everyone who had wanted to make a run at me was done. Of course, the problem with that theory was that I'd be looking over my shoulder for the rest of my life wondering if someone was going to sneak up and shoot me in the back of the head with a pistol, but it was where I was at.

Everybody had dumped on me today. People had tried to kill me, my own government/previous employer had disgraced me in front of the world, even my scum-sucking lawyers had quit on me, and it was highly doubtful that anyone was going to come knocking to hire me now that I—

I blinked, sitting there thinking. Someone had already come to visit, and I'd forgotten. Timothy Logan, that little snake, had come to my office and prostrated himself to me, trying to hire me. I furrowed my brow in concentration, some of my anger with him past. What was it he'd said? That there was more going on with Palleton Labs than we'd known?

I didn't have anything else to do, and my phone was charging anyway, so I decided to do a little research while I waited. I typed "Palleton Labs" into the search bar of my phone's browser and waited. It would have been a lot faster to do the search on my computer, but McCartney had risen to a basic enough level of competence to trash it.

When the results popped up, I hit the first one, which was a basic press release about Palleton's opening in Portland's suburbs. I skimmed it, but it was pretty boilerplate stuff about ribbon-cutting and other associated bullshit, with a photo of some douchebag slicing his way through a ribbon with a comically large pair of scissors.

I stopped.

I knew that douchebag.

"What the hell is Edward Cavanagh doing cutting the

ribbon for this place?" I asked, as though someone might just answer out of thin air. I looked down below, and sure enough, the caption confirmed it: "Edward Cavanagh and Palleton Labs inaugurate new era in biotech research in Portland."

I picked my phone up and dialed immediately, and as soon as J.J. answered, I said, "Edward Cavanagh was tied into Palleton Labs somehow."

"Why, hello to you, too," J.J. said. "It's such a pleasure to talk to you, Sienna."

"Seriously, did you hear me?" I asked.

"I was just trying to remind you of manners," he said.

"Fuck manners," I said. "This is important."

"We'll just skip the part about speaking like a lady, then," J.J. said. "Also, I needed my computer to boot, so … ah. Palleton Labs, yes, okay. I'm not seeing it on my list of Cavanagh-funded entities."

"Yeah, but your list missed NITU in Chicago, too, didn't it?" I asked. "Just search the internet for Palleton Labs and the first damned result that pops up is Cavanagh cutting the ribbon at that place."

He was quiet for a minute. "Hmmm. Well. That's interesting, isn't it?"

I tried to control my anger, because getting mad at him was pointless. "This guy has been dead for over a year. How is it we're still not clear on how many pies he had his fingers in?"

"Because we're not health inspectors?"

"J.J.!"

"Because he was a billionaire, Sienna, with a capital B and lots of capital. You ever try and track a billionaire's dough? Because I've tried, and if the Panama Papers proved anything, it's that the governments of the world pretty much have no clue how to, either."

"But this isn't even that difficult!" I said, frustration pouring out. "I mean, it's the first item in an internet search on the subject!"

"Yeah, but it's not even in the first thousand on Cavanagh himself," J.J. said. "Look, I wrote an algorithm to send spiders across the web searching for references to him—"

"You did what with spiders and webs?"

"I—never mind. The point is, I tried to track down all the places his money went, and I approached it from a few different angles, but Sienna—I'm one guy, and this dude had an army of people investing his money for him. They worked their asses off obscuring the trail of cash Cavanagh invested before he died, and I'm pretty sure someone came along ex post facto and did some mopping up, too. Probably employed through some law firm to keep a lid on his involvement with some of these smaller ventures so they didn't get hit with negative press after what he did in Atlanta."

"Someone talking about Cavanagh over here?" Augustus asked in the background.

"Yeah, Sienna found out that lab you guys hit in Portland was opened by Cavanagh," J.J. said, stopping to explain. "You know, I'm just gonna put you on speaker."

"Oooh, the plot thickens," Augustus said, sounding like he was kind of windblown. I hate speakerphone.

"It's actually still fairly thin, I think," I said. "Because we have no idea what Palleton was doing in that vault."

"Well, Cavanagh already figured out how to bestow meta powers and take them away with chemicals," Augustus said. "And that guy he funded in Chicago was working on killing us all, so … what haven't we covered on the bio research spectrum?"

"How to turn you all into phenomenal dancers?" J.J. asked.

"Pffft, I'm already a phenomenal dancer," Augustus said.

"Phenomenal tap dancers?" J.J. asked.

"Shit, yo, Gregory Hines was like a hero to me in my youth," Augustus said. "I took classes for six years." There was a thumping noise that I presumed was him trying to show his stuff. "Well, I can't really do it in these kicks, but you get the point."

"My point," I said, "is that we just keep getting more and more tiebacks to this guy, and he's dead. How many biotech concerns did he touch in this country?"

"He is like the Midas of biotech crap we keep running across," Augustus said.

"Or like the spider at the middle of this really big web, to keep with the earlier theme." I couldn't be sure whose voice that was, but it sounded a little like Abigail.

"Or like—"

"Enough with the similes," I said. "Bottom line, I want to know what was going on at Palleton Labs. How do we find out?"

"Mmm, I could try and hack them, I guess," J.J. said. "Give me an hour and I'll give you a call back?"

I frowned. "Is it really going to take you an hour?"

"I dunno," he said, yawning, "I'm kinda tired. Was thinking about taking a nap." Abigail muttered something in the background. "Well, *we* were. Together, you know." He paused. "You know, a siesta. Together. So we can—"

"If you make it any more obvious, J.J.," I said, "you might as well just film it and put it on Pornhub for people to enjoy. Or not enjoy, as the case may be."

"Oh, they'd enjoy it," Abigail said.

"Oh. My. Lawd." Augustus sounded pained.

"Do you really need this right now, like *right now*—or are you just bored?" he asked.

I blinked, holding in the explosion. Blowing up at him would be pointless, because really, what was I going to do with this info? I couldn't fly to Portland to follow up on anything he found, after all, unless I went commercial, and I was trying—oh so hard—not to alienate J.J., who was overall a good guy and a good worker and a helpful overall member of the team, even though he was trying oh so hard himself to step on my patience at the moment. "Hurry, J.J.," I said. "Please."

"Uh, oh, um … okay," he said, probably taken aback that I was exercising politeness. "Bye, then."

"Good bye," I said, and let him hang up first.

I sagged back in my chair, trying to decide how I should have handled that. I could have yelled, could have screamed, could have done the normal Sienna thing and threatened violence.

But I'd done all that, for years and years, and where had it gotten me?

Sitting in an empty office, alone, with the only people I could count on half a country away and reporters lined up outside my door like piranhas, waiting to strip every morsel of meat from my body if they got half a chance. The federal government waiting, poised like an axe over the back of my neck, led by an ex of mine so pissed at me that I really believed he'd happily look me in the eye and gun me down.

What had gotten me here wouldn't get me any farther, that much I knew. So I sat there, feeling pretty damned powerless, just waiting. The sun started to sink in the sky, shadows getting long on the walls, and I waited, hoping that someone would give me a way to save myself from sinking.

25.

For variety, the network I was watching brought on Owen Traverton for an interview, because I guess trashing me was pretty much the national pastime at the moment, and I felt almost nauseous enough to throw up. I thought about going out front, setting the record straight—about what Traverton had done in his masquerade as my dog, about the crimes of Thunder Hayes, Bronson McCartney, and Louis Terry. Hayes was a straight-up long-term criminal. McCartney was a murderer. Terry was a pedophile, and a disgusting one. Even before he started ruining my life I wished I'd killed him.

Yet something inside me knew instinctively what would happen if I went out there and tried to defend myself. Maybe it was experience with the mauling I took in my first interview, but it was like I sensed sharks in the water just outside my office walls. These reporters didn't like me. They looked down on me, held me in contempt, and I had this feeling that walking out that front door and facing my problems like my first instinct suggested would do little more than deliver all my watching enemies another victory. Because, really, how was I supposed to explain away the accusations that President Harmon had just made? "Oh, no, I totally didn't kill anyone who really deserved it because they murdered my boyfriend." I wasn't a convincing enough liar to pull that one off.

My phone rang again, and I frowned at it. It was Kat, according to the caller ID, which was weird. Hesitantly, and only because I thought maybe J.J. had fried his battery and borrowed Kat's to make the call, I answered. "Hello?"

"Oh my gosh, Sienna, I just saw," Kat gushed, doing that thing where she sounds genuinely sorry to have heard your bad news. "Are you okay? How are you holding up?"

"Ariadne's brandy bottle got broken in McCartney's sack of our office, so I'm not doing that well," I said, just letting the honesty flow out.

"It's so terrible," Kat said. "They're just destroying you on every network. I mean, just when I think things can't get any more horrible, the freaking president goes and tears you a new vaj live on national television."

"Yes, I noticed," I said, wishing she would stop rubbing it in. Actually, what I really wished for was to draw Shadow and just start shooting the TV.

My phone buzzed, heralding the arrival of a text message. I lifted it up and stared at the screen. My eyes nearly bulged out as I stared.

It was from Steven Clayton, famous Hollywood actor at large. *On location in Australia and just heard the news. Don't let the bastards get you down. You still have supporters out there, no matter how they try and trash you.*

"Hello?" Kat trilled. "Sienna, are you there?"

"Sorry," I said. "I got a text from Steven Clayton, believe it or not. He, um … was sending his support." I felt a very strange wash of shame mingled with guilt. I'd done what Harmon had accused me of, yet still I had people like poor Steven believing that I was innocent. Maybe he was projecting on to me.

"Of course he was," Kat said, without a hint of jealousy. I knew she'd been interested in Steven herself, since I'd run across him for the first time while helping Kat avoid being killed by Redbeard out in LA. "He's a good guy. And Sienna … you're one of the good guys. Errr, good girl. Wait, no … good girl kind of has a different connotation than good guy, doesn't it? Being a good girl is so last century. You're a bad girl, Sienna. In the best way."

"Thanks … I think?" I wasn't quite sure how to take that, because for once, Kat had gotten a step or two ahead of me.

"When people give you shit," Kat said, "you don't do what

I do and just passively sit by and try and spin it into gold. Which sucks, by the way. I feel like I'm just sitting there, my mouth full of shit sandwich, trying to grin for the cameras. When someone gives you shit, you take it and cram it down their throat, not even bothering to smile until you've done it. Then you grin, because ha ha, they totally deserved that. I wish I were brave like you because I'm sick of taking peoples' shit. I was sick of taking Taggert's shit until you came along and reminded me that I didn't have to. You don't let people push you around, Sienna. Don't start now."

"*People* aren't pushing me around," I said. "The US government is, and mostly to stop me from, uhm … viciously revenging myself on people who have wronged me."

"That's boloney," Kat said. "President Harmon is pushing you around. The press is pushing you around. They're ripping you up, and you know damned well if you try and defend yourself, most of them are going to continue crapping all over you because it's good ratings. The whole country knows you. A lot of people like you. Heroes falling? It's like the gold star in their business, the number one thing they love to cover—scandal. And this is a scandal. Let me contact my PR firm in LA, see what they can do to turn this around for you."

I felt strangely touched. This was Kat. Kat was eager to help me. "Thank you," I said, feeling a little choked up.

"It's gonna be okay, Sienna," she said, calm and reassuring. "We're going to get through this. Together, all right?"

"All right," I said, and she clicked off the other end of the line. I sat there in the growing darkness, staring at the TV screen, but not a bit of it sank in on me, because I was still just sitting there, floored, at the fact that Kat—Kat, of all people—was my shining light in the darkness.

26.

I traded text messages with Steven Clayton for a while, and took a quick call from Hampton, who was sitting in Chicago and worried for me. I'll spare you the mush, but it was a long talk, filled with deep pauses, and didn't conclude until after the sun was down and the sound of the nearby road had faded somewhat. The reporters seemed to have gotten quiet. I could still hear them prepping for their next segments, but only a few were on the air at a time, and the breathless coverage of my office's facade had given way to news reports about other goings-on in the world. Which was good, because there was a massacre going on in a third-world country across the globe, and not one going on in my parking lot, so it felt like it was only fair for them to at least report on that for thirty seconds per hour. The damned vultures.

Another text lit up my phone. *Heard about your troubles. I hope it's not true what they say you did, but just as you backed me, know I'm your corner.* It was from Jamie Barton, and she'd signed it *Gravity.* I guess the copyright lawyers hadn't gotten to her for that one yet.

I stood, my back and legs a little stiff. I thumped a booted foot up on the table and leaned over to stretch. As a meta, my muscles didn't really get tight, but I felt the need to move, to do something, anything. The TV was on, but I was ignoring it to the best of my ability.

The phone buzzed again, and I scooped it up. *J.J.,* read the screen, and I answered, "Give me happy news."

"Well …" J.J. said, sounding pained, "that might be tough."

I held in my disappointment. "Shit." Okay. I didn't hold it in that well.

"Palleton Labs is an interesting little conundrum," J.J. said. "I managed to get past their firewall, but there's almost nothing there."

I waited for him to make himself clear, but apparently he was waiting for me to ask a question. "Whatever do you mean?" I obliged.

"There's like, twenty computers on the network behind their firewall. I looked at the satellite overheads of that place, and I have to believe they've got more than twenty employees there."

"Agreed," I said.

"Sooo," he said, "I think what we've got going on here is a black network."

"Racist!" Augustus called from somewhere in the background.

"I—no, that's not what I—I totally did not mean— seriously, guy, I—" J.J. sputtered.

"Dude, I'm messing with you," Augustus said, getting a little clearer. "You're such an easy mark. You know what I mean?"

"He really is," Abigail said in the background. "Because he's a sweetie."

I suppressed my gag reflex. "So you're saying the rest of the network is offline?"

J.J. sounded impressed. "Uh, yeah. It's either that, or they don't have more than twenty computers."

"They've got a vault that takes up a lot of real estate on the top floor," I said, "and it's meta proof. A Gavrikov couldn't get through it, and we burn pretty hot. So …"

"They're into the secrets business," J.J. said. "Seems likely they'd take their INFOSEC pretty seriously."

"Uh huh," I said, sitting down in my chair and leaning back again. "So … anything of use from the computers you could access?"

"One person has a really, really serious porn habit that I

think they need to address," J.J. said, "and I found the company financials. Not on the same computer. Ms. Porn Habit seems like she's probably the admin supervisor, but the financials guy only had cat photos on his hard drive, other than his work stuff—"

"Fascinating," I said, though it really wasn't. "What do the financials say?"

"Nothing," J.J. said, and then he laughed, "You have to read them!" He guffawed for a minute, then settled down. "That joke always kills me."

"It's a classic for a reason," Abigail said, apparently feeding his ego. I guess he could use it.

"Anyway, Ariadne took a peek," J.J. said, "and she claims that whoever does their finances should probably be in prison for fraud. Poor guy. He's not gonna see any cat photos in there—"

"Why?" I asked, cutting right to it.

"Well, I'm pretty sure it's because he wouldn't get much internet time to look at cat pics in prison—"

"Why did Ariadne say the financials are fraudulent?" I asked, doing a remarkable job of restraining myself. Old Sienna would have gone nuclear about six annoying asides ago.

"Oh, because they don't disclose what a lot of the expenditures are for," he said. "She basically called it a blind man's budget, where you'd get more information reading it if you—if you couldn't see it, I guess? I dunno, I think she might have overreached with that analogy, what do you th—"

"I think I'm in the position of knowing that Timothy Logan and his crime bros were right," I said.

"And crime sisses," Augustus added helpfully.

"There's something funky going on at Palleton Labs," I said. "And since it's all offline, I guess I'm not getting in to take a peek unless—"

"You actually go there and take a peek, yeah," J.J. said. "That was the conclusion I came to, too. So … you taking a trip to Portland, then? Road trip, obvs, because you can't fly anymore?"

"Thanks for rubbing that in," I said. "And no. I have other concerns at the moment."

"Uh, yeah," Augustus said, sounding a little awestruck in the background, "you do."

"Yes," I said, trying to decide where he was going with that, "I'd—"

"No, Sienna," Augustus said, and there was a stir of movement, "are you near a TV?"

"Yeah," I said, glancing up, "wh—"

I stopped mid-sentence as my eyes caught on the image on screen. There was a blazing fire, a hellscape of a burning building. It was utterly consumed, flames pouring from the roofline, an inferno leaping into the sky. I stood immediately, instinctively, wondering where it was, and if I could get there in time to save whoever—

But, no. I couldn't fly. I relaxed a millimeter, that feeling of perpetual sickness infusing my stomach once more as I realized all the responsibilities of saving people all over the place were off my shoulders. I almost sat back down—

But then I realized that the building looked entirely too familiar.

The fire reached past trees, scorching their bare branches, which had already been bare before the fire licked at them. I knew, because I'd seen the leaves fall myself just a few weeks earlier. I peered at the blaze, and there in the front I could see the hole in the living room window where the Clarys had come crashing in only twenty-four hours ago, disturbing me in the middle of my margarita pity party.

"Oh no," I whispered, and dropped the phone, barely catching it with my meta reflexes before it hit the ground.

I knew that place, that place that was burning.

It was my house.

27.

"Please just let me through," I said, trying to push my way past a throng of reporters shoving microphones in my face. It felt like I could smell fire, even though I'd only just left the office a minute earlier. I'd had to call for an Uber, because I couldn't fly, even though it would have gotten me there in a matter of seconds. No, I had to stay on the ground, because to do otherwise would have been against the laws of man and nature, but only one of them was actively trying to bring me down at the moment.

"Ms. Nealon, how do you respond to the president's allegations of—"

"Are you a murderer?"

"Sienna, what do you think of the dress that Jennifer Lopez wore to the Academy Awards?"

I swear that last one was a real question. I squeezed into the back seat of a Prius and shut the door, and the driver shot off before anyone could get in front of her.

"Damn," she said, looking in her rearview. "That was something, huh?"

"Tell me about it," I said, looking at her eyes in the rearview. They were dark, and so was her complexion. Her hair was a different story, though, blond as blond could get, which looked like a lovely contrast to her deep chocolate skin tone. It was short, and frizzed into an afro. A blond, short afro. I tried not to stare, but it was kinda cool.

"So, we're heading to 832 Hamilton Ave?"

"Yeah," I said. "Expect a similar crowd when we arrive."

"Are you famous or something?" she asked, looking back at me again.

I looked at myself in the rearview. I looked paler than usual, dark circles under my eyes. "Or something, yeah." Infamous felt more accurate.

"I feel like I recognize you from somewhere," she said, and she pursed her lips as she considered it.

"Do you watch the news?" I prepared myself, in case I got kicked out of my Uber.

"Nope," she said. "Nothing on there but shit and more shit. If I want to feel bad about life I'll go to talk to my brother for a while, you know what I mean?"

"Boy, do I," I said. "Anyway … let's just say I've been on the news today, and not in a great way."

"Aww, that sucks. What happened?"

"Nothing. At least not lately," I said. "This stuff … it's all like ancient history to me."

"Oh, yeah? When did it happen?"

"Five, six years ago?" I tried to do the math in my head as we hit 212 and headed east. "Feels like forever."

"It ain't easy, outrunning the past," she said, nodding along like that was sage wisdom. It kind of was.

"Tell me about it," I said and we fell into silence.

The ride was simultaneously forever and over in a minute, the trees on 212 blurring past at first, and then we merged with 62, and we were making the turn onto 35W north in a flash. Pretty soon we were exiting, and I could hear the sirens in the distance, see the cloud of black smoke against the light pollution of my neighborhood, the orange blaze lighting up the night.

I had the driver drop me just before my street and I ran the last few hundred yards. There was a crowd in front of my house, fire trucks just pulling up as I got there. A whole crowd of reporters and apparently no one had bothered to call 911. I guess they figured someone else was doing it.

I pushed through the crowd, lightly as could. "Let me through, please," I said, trying to be polite. My words were wracked with desperation. I wanted to fly, high up, get this done. The house was just burning, the roof completely engulfed, flames coming out of the windows. I took a deep breath as I shoved to the fore, and readied myself, ready to pull the fire out and snuff it—

A hand like steel clamped on my upper arm, and I wheeled about, ready to unleash on whoever was attacking me. The grip disappeared after my assailant had spun me around, his ruddy face lit by fire, smug, taunting, like a miniature Harmon, though he was far more familiar than that. "Don't," Scott Byerly said, and his tone was all warning, audible over the roaring of the flames.

"I'm putting out a fire," I said, and turned away from him. *Gavrikov,* I said in my own mind, *time to*—

Scott grabbed me again, pulling me a step back, and I let him because I was putting all my effort into not hitting him hard enough to break his face and neck in one punch. "I'm a federal agent," he said, as though I didn't know this, "and this is a crime scene. If you interfere in it, I will arrest you."

"Interfere?" I stared at him, his face shadowed and orange where the flames lit it. "This is my house. I just want to put it out—"

"No," he said, and he smiled, just slightly. Friday eased up behind him, arms crossed, a grin of his own visible in the mask hole. "Don't disturb the scene until our forensics people get a chance to go over it. It could be arson."

"And how is arson a federal crime?" I asked. Somehow I wasn't furious. I was crushed, brittle, feeling broken.

"Oh, the arson isn't," he said, and he leered at me, looking positively demonic in his joy at my sorrow. "I'm talking about your house. Your house is a federal crime scene." He pulled a piece of paper out of his pocket. "This is a search warrant, and it *was* going to be executed tonight." He glanced to the side, still smiling smugly. "We're going to be looking into your culpability in this."

"I'm no special investigator," Friday said, taunting, "but it seems to me this fire might have been set to hide something."

"Who would have motive for that?" Scott asked, but there was no doubt showing in who he believed responsible.

"I've been in my office all day," I said, feeling even more

slack, suddenly, like I was going to melt from the heat, become an artifact, slag left on my lawn.

"Any witnesses can corroborate that?" Scott asked. He was still smiling, damn him.

"No," I said. I'd been out of sight pretty much all day, and they knew how fast I could fly if I was of a mind to.

"I didn't think so," Scott said. "You should stick around." He nodded at the fire. "After it's over … we're going to want to ask you some questions." And he took a few steps back.

I shouldn't have felt conflicted, I thought as I watched the house burn, the flames dipping lower and lower as they ran out of fuel to consume. This house had been my prison for over a decade. There was still a metal box in the basement where I'd been confined, locked up.

But it was the last thing I had of my mother's.

It was where I kept everything I owned.

It was my home.

And I watched helplessly as it burned, the fire department not arriving until there was nearly nothing left but ashes, the heat fading as the flame diminished, leaving me standing alone on a smoky street in Minneapolis on a cold autumn night.

28.

They kept me on the scene for hours, and I let them. What else was I going to do? Scream? Hit them? Fly off into the sky as I flung middle fingers at all of them? Tempting as that would have been, I contained myself and just sat there, chilled, without so much as a jacket, the smoke heavy in the air and the occasional hiss and pop from the ashes barely audible over the constant questions shouted at me from behind the yellow police "CRIME SCENE" tape.

"Ms. Nealon! Did you have anything to do with the burning of your house?"

"Do you have any comment on the accusations of prisoner abuse that have been leveled against you by your former inmates?"

"Sienna, what do you think of Drake's new single?"

"Who the hell gave that guy press credentials?" I wondered aloud as I stood on my lawn, having just weathered a snotty and condescending interview conducted by Scott and Friday, in which Friday had once more revealed why he was not the brains of this operation or any other.

Scott had been worse, though. He'd asked his questions—dull formalities of the "Where were you two hours ago?" sort—with a nasty indifference bordering on gleeful depravity at my suffering. I didn't engage with him any more than I had to, letting him have his moment of ghoulish, joyful triumph at my tragedy. It was just a house, I kept telling myself. The people I cared about were safe, after all, so what did a house matter, anyway?

It was still a tough sell.

They told me to wait right where they left me, then came back and asked the same questions again. I answered them again, in just as dull a tone of voice, with just as little care for how I sounded. Friday guffawed every time arson was mentioned, but I could tell they had nothing on me. They were just being porn-star-sized dicks.

Still, I stayed after they finished their second round of questions because they asked me to. I just shrugged and did it. I didn't know where this was going, and I didn't care. I had nowhere else to be. Even if they'd cut me loose, where was I going to go? My office? What fun, being surrounded by more inane press inquiries.

No one talked to me. Not the fire department, not the paramedics, not the Minneapolis cops on the scene. I didn't blame any of them; Scott and Friday were looking at me sullenly from across the yard, Scott on his cell phone, probably getting instructions from the mothership—a.k.a., Andrew Phillips—and none of the locals wanted to get on their bad side.

I didn't really want to be on their bad side, either, but here I was, so … shit happens, I guess.

What now? Zack asked gently in my head.

Bloody vengeance, Wolfe growled.

"No," I said, turning back to the smoky embers, so the press wouldn't see me talking to myself. The stories would write themselves.

We don't know who did this, Bjorn said, sounding for a brief moment like the voice of reason. *We should find them. And then, bloody vengeance.*

"Knew that reason wasn't going to last."

There are rules, people, Roberto Bastian said. *She's got big brother's eyes all over her. Revenge, right now? Bad idea.*

Revenge is always a good idea, Bjorn said.

Revenge is only a good idea if you can get away with it, Eve said darkly. *Recall, she's even now in trouble for our murders.* I saw a flash of a leer from her. *I hope you go to jail for those, by the way.*

"Thanks."

Then we will be in jail as well, fool, Gavrikov said. *Have you any idea how boring prison is?*

Especially the kind they'll put her into, Zack said, oh-so-helpfully reminding me that whatever consequences came my way, they'd be special. *She'll be lucky if she talks to a normal person again for the rest of her life. And forget about getting a TV.*

Mmm, that would be boring, Eve said. *All right, I change my mind. I hope you get away with killing us, but only because I don't wish to be bored beyond death.*

"So gracious."

These prisoners are a threat, Wolfe said, sounding unusually serious. He could be playful, forceful, and malignant, all in turn. But this Wolfe sounded worried. *This is not just a matter of vengeance; it is a matter of security. They are doing things like this, burning down the house ... the message is clear. The government will not protect her. They want her to die.*

That's a bit of a stretch, Zack said.

If they wanted her dead, Bastian said, *she would be dead. The government has operatives that could make that happen so fast, she wouldn't even see it coming.*

"Weeeeee," I muttered.

It's true, Eve said. *They don't want to be connected to this. But if she dies by the hand of one of the prisoners ...*

I think you call that plausible deniability, Gavrikov said. *They get what they want without getting their hands dirty. It even smells of poetic justice for the festering press of your country.*

Wow, Zack said, *now I am really, really sorry I voted for Gerry Harmon that first time when he was up for VP.*

He seemed charming, Eve said. *You know. For a man.*

We need to focus on the threat, Wolfe said, sounding increasingly desperate. *We need to kill these—*

"We can't kill them," I said. "Not without bringing the whole government down on our—on my—head."

Sienna, Wolfe said, and now he was so out of sorts he didn't growl. He pleaded. *I know you don't want to hear this ... but it's time.*

I frowned, cool air prickling my scalp. "Time for what?"

Time to put aside this genteel dream of being a soft little person walking around like any other, Wolfe said. *You are not like everyone else. You never have been.*

I glanced over my shoulder. The crowd was still there, behind the police tape, and the fire department was watching me with the cops, all quiet and subdued, like they were afraid I'd lose my shit and murder them all. I turned back so no one could see my lips move. "I'm a person like anyone else, Wolfe. I'm part of society and bound by its laws—"

No, you aren't, he said. You are different. *You have always been different. You are a descendant of Death, his own blood, his heir,* Wolfe hissed. *They are the sheep that wait to be culled, and you are playing shepherd when you should take your rightful place as—*

"Wolf?"

Goddess. He growled, a sound low in the throat he no longer had. *You have the blood of a deity, and you were made to rule, given power over life and death and soul. You are better than them— and you always have been. Take the step forward. Show them your strength. Make them see who you are. Defy them, and rip out the hearts of all who defy you, shoving them, still-beating, down their throats—*

"That's about enough of that," I said.

No, Wolfe said, *it is not. Most of them will die in their beds, never being any more than cattle passing through this world. You have a destiny. You could become more than they would ever dream of. The power is there, it's yours for the taking. All you need do is reach out your hand—*

"No." I looked down at my hand. It was shaking, just slightly. "I'm *not* death. I'm not made to rule." I looked at the damage fire had wrought to my home, and thought about all the places where destruction had followed me in my travels. "I'm not Sovereign, and I don't believe this world would be a better place by having me in charge of it." I snorted and caught a glimpse of Scott out of the corner of my eye, surly and barking something at Friday about "making it happen." "I can't even rule my own life without making it a wreck, Wolfe. How am I supposed to rule anyone else?"

You could. You could if you wanted to.

"I don't want to," I whispered as Scott crossed over to me, moisture pulling out of the sodden ground to follow him, lit by all the floodlights and casting a bizarre rainbow in his wake. It occurred to me, finally, that he could have put out the fire in my house if he'd wanted to, too.

And he chose not to because he hated me.

"You're free to go," he said roughly, "but we'll be—"

"Watching, yes," I said. "By the way, do you know where the FAA's authority starts over the skies?"

He froze, a half second away from stalking off, caught by my unexpected question. "No. Wh—"

"Pretty sure it's at least a hundred feet up," I said, and before he could yell at me not to, I jumped, a long, mostly horizontal leap that kept me beneath the power lines. I soared over the heads of the assembled press, cleared a whole block, and came down at the end of the street, right at the corner. I turned back, let them see me—let them see that no, I wasn't flying, or violating FAA rules, and then I jumped again, and again, and again, heading away from my old neighborhood faster than the press or Scott or anyone else could follow me.

Because I didn't have any reason left to be there.

29.

I bellied up to the bar in a place a little off the beaten path. I had kept jumping until I reached Bloomington, which was south of home and east of work, and finally stopped when I saw a local watering hole with a neon sign and only a handful of cars in the parking lot. It wasn't quite a dive, but it was close. The fact there were only five people inside cemented my decision.

"What'll you have?" the bartender asked. He looked older, probably early fifties, hair grey everywhere he still had it, a default scowl on his face that didn't exactly scream, "Welcome!"

"Tequila," I decided. It wasn't like I needed to be able to drive. "Give me three shots."

If this request came as a surprise to him, he didn't show it, and he poured three shot glasses full as I put some cash on the bar along with my cell phone.

The bartender concluded his triple pour, scooped the cash, eyed my cell phone, and said, "Ariadne's calling you."

I already had a shot in my hand, and downed it. "Of course she is," I said after I finished getting down the tequila. It burned a little.

He shrugged and wandered off, turning his attention to a couple roughly his own age that had a hard look about them, like they'd been drinking a lot for a long time. One of them laughed at something he said as he came over to them, but neither of them gave me so much as a look of interest. Based on the bartender's demeanor, he might have forgotten I had even walked in by the way he stood there, engaging with them.

Someone slid onto the stool next to me, and I looked up to see another older guy, one of the remaining two people in the joint put his beer down. "Mind if I sit here?" he asked. He had a pretty neutral look, was probably at least a decade older than the bartender, but lacked the scowl. "Nothing untoward intended, young lady, I just thought maybe you'd like a conversation."

"Sure, knock yourself out," I said, picking up my second shot and pondering it, turning to look for the last patron. She was in the corner, probably about one drink from passed out, head on the table and talking to herself. I stared at her hard, but she had her eyes closed, and I knew after a moment that she wasn't anyone I knew, and probably wasn't an assassin with a grudge, waiting to kill me.

"What brings you in tonight?" the man next to me asked. "I'm Ronald, by the way."

"Clearly it's the festive atmosphere," I snarked, downing the second shot. This one burned slightly less on the way down. Maybe I was getting used to it. "It's just a crazy party up in here."

Ronald chortled. "It's like this most weeknights. Did you want to be left alone?"

"I'm pretty ambivalent about it," I said, shrugging broadly. My phone rattled on the bar, ringing again. *Ariadne*, the screen read again. I pushed the button and sent it to voicemail. It wasn't personal; I just didn't figure having Ariadne check in on me right now would lead to anything good. *Oh, hi, Ariadne, I'm at a bar on my second shot of tequila. What's up with you?*

"Looks like you've missed a few calls from this Ariadne," Ronald Probably Not McDonald said, and I didn't look at him. I slid my third shot in front of me and contemplated just gunning it back now. "Friend of yours?"

"Something like that," I said.

"Uhh ... girlfriend?" he probed about as delicately as a drunken me, if I'd been of a mind to do any probing. "Not that there's—"

"No," I said, "she doesn't have a girlfriend right now. Why does that even mat—"

"I'm just—asking questions," Ronald said, backpedaling so fast I was surprised his metaphorical bike didn't fall over. "Curious, you know. I was in sales for years and years, and—"

"Are you going to try and sell me something?" I asked, giving him evil side-eye.

"I'm retired," he said with a low chuckle. "Got nothing left to sell, and nothing but time to fill … which is why I'm here tonight."

"I see," I said. "I, too, suddenly find myself with time to fill."

"Oh, are you retired?" He said it coyly, like he was being funny.

"I might just be," I said. I downed the last shot, taking care not to smash the glass on the bar when I was done. I could have done it, too, sending shards showering over everyone in the place. "Hell if I know."

"So … you're having job problems?" he asked, a little less clumsily. It was also possible the tequila was kicking in on my side of the conversation and making him seem just a little smoother.

"I'm having every kind of problem you can imagine, Ronald Not-Weasley."

He frowned. "Uhhh … not Weasl—"

"Never mind," I said, wondering if I should order more shots. It seemed like a good idea, but it was also possible my judgment was already shot to hell by the alcohol. "You come here a lot, then?"

He nodded. "I try not to more than once a week or so. I'm afraid it might be habit forming to be in here every night." He cast a look down the bar to the couple that was jawing with the bartender, then another to the woman with her head on the table in the corner.

"I was never much of a drinker," I said, turning on my stool to face him, suddenly full of bubbly exuberance and excited to share my opinions with him. "I mean, I'd have one every once in a while, but … I don't know. I didn't need to. I could take it or leave it. But see, I know other people do, and I never got that. Like I knew people came into places like this and did this shit every night ... one time I arrested this guy—"

"You a cop?" he asked.

I plunged on, barely noticing he'd spoken. "—and it was so sad, Ronald, he was passed out in his easy chair with a case of beer. Apparently he bought one every night of the week, and his only goal in life was to transfer the full cans on one side of his chair to the garbage on the other side. He had just—" I made a motion with my hands, spreading them really wide, "—just bags and bags of empty beer cans. I never got that, really. Never understood it." I motioned the bartender over, but he didn't see me because he was popping a fresh beer for the couple that were his bestest buds. "Until now."

"And what do you know now?" he asked.

"That if I felt this fucking powerless in the world all the time," I said, wondering if I was going to have break the bartender's skull open or throw a flame burst past his face to get his attention, "I'd be drunk every hour of every day."

I gave Ronald a look, since I wasn't having any luck getting the bartender's attention, but he looked ... sad. Like he pitied me. "Whatever bad time you're going through, it won't last—"

"I don't really care anymore," I said, giving up on getting another tequila. "I've done some bad things. Some good ones, too, probably, but those don't really matter. Because just the same as someone can tell me ten good things about me and I forget them all as soon as someone says one terrible thing about me ... it's just the same for our deeds. The good we do doesn't matter, because we're so dark and negative that no one will ever forget the wrongs we've done."

"What wrongs have you done?" Ronald asked, in a hushed whisper.

I felt cold, and nothing but. "The worst you can imagine." I watched him shudder, and I guessed he was imagining it. "Take care, Ronald." And I bailed, walking out the front door into the freezing ass cold. The temp had dropped when the sun went down, winter coming on hard. It was probably in the forties, autumn chill biting at my fingers and making me shiver as I walked outside.

"I don't need this," I said to myself. What exactly it was I didn't need, I wasn't real clear on. It wasn't an articulate thought, after all, more of a feeling. Like I was getting a raw deal, even though in my heart I knew ...

... I probably wasn't getting anything I didn't truly deserve.

"Screw it," I decided and started walking. There was a gravel parking lot, and past that, a sidewalk. I wasn't quite staggering, but I was definitely swaying, and I headed for the sidewalk, figuring that walking for a little bit was a better idea than leaping through the air all drunk and willy-nilly.

I was a step away from the sidewalk when I heard the crack of the rifle. The bullet hit less than a second later, splattering the gravel in front of me as it blew out of my sternum. It didn't knock me over, but I still felt the hit, like somebody had just driven a javelin right through my chest.

A little spurt of blood followed, then another, with each beat of my heart. Someone had shot me right through it, I realized, as the ground came rushing up to me. I hit, hard, and had enough consciousness left to realize that I'd just been ambushed before the darkness started to close in around me, taking me into its cold, unforgiving embrace.

30.

In the dimness around me, I could feel my heart laboring to pump; I was pretty sure a lot of its musculature had been blown out of my chest by the rifle shot. I was curled on the ground in the fetal position, wishing I could just hug my knees to me and make the pain stop, to get the fading light to just go out. It was cold, so cold, and I didn't have a jacket, and that seemed so important as the darkness crawled in at the corners of my vision.

Sienna, hang on, Wolfe said, sounding more urgent than I could recall hearing him in some time.

Sienna, stay awake! Zack yelled, the voice in my head so loud it caused my hair to tickle down to my scalp, to stand on its ends. *You're under attack.*

Another shot echoed through the night and hit me in the back, lower right hand side. My kidney exploded and I gasped in pain, writhing. There was no cover nearby, and I hurt so much I couldn't think straight.

We must move her, Gavrikov said, and I lifted off the ground. My body was so overwhelmed with pain that it was shutting down my mind, but not the minds that were with me. They'd taken control of me before, back when I was weaker, but not of late. I floated through the air, not gently, and crashed behind a fence, almost slamming into a telephone pole. I came to rest in a thick patch of damp grass that felt like little frozen ice crystals brushing my cheek.

I cannot move her any farther, Gavrikov said, sounding exhausted. *I am fighting her body, and it is too much.*

Hang on, Wolfe grunted. *I'm fighting her body, too, but it's healing … slowly.*

Shot through the heart, Eve said, almost sadly. *Is this how it's to end, then?*

"No," I whispered, then clenched my teeth together. I tightened my chest muscles, and a line of blood slopped down my front, thinner than it had been a moment ago. My back was pure agony where the second shot had landed, and I looked down. My shirt was slick and dark in the thin light of the lamp atop the telephone pole.

"Get to her!" someone shouted in the distance. It was a woman's voice. "Before she heals!"

"You got her in the heart," came another voice, this one a man's. They were both familiar. "She's not healing from that."

"You don't know that," the woman said. "We aren't familiar enough with whatever meta gave her that power to make the call."

"Fine, have it your way," he said. "She flew low, barely off the ground, looking half dead." He paused, and when he spoke again, he sounded downright gleeful. "Police are already on the way, probably, right? Or do you think a couple gunshots could go unnoticed in this part of Bloomington?"

The woman's voice was drawing closer. "The cops are probably on their way. Why?"

"No reason." I heard a click, and then a light grunt, and something landed a few feet away from me, thumping on the dirt. I lifted my dazed head.

GRENADE! Bastian shouted in my mind, and I didn't have time to react before it went off.

It wasn't all fire like in the movies. It made a loud popping noise, and I felt about a thousand massive pinpricks of pain as the shrapnel tore through me. It hit the bottom of my feet, got me in the forehead and cheeks, my shoulders. The blast wasn't world-ending, but it damned sure felt like it, rolling me over and causing my head to ring like the Liberty Bell.

Or not, since no one rings the Liberty Bell anymore.

I opened an eye and saw another little object thump down next to me, much closer this time. I raised a shaking, bloody hand, helplessly.

Nein! Eve Kappler shouted, and three flashes of light burst out of my palm, wrapping the grenade tightly, making it look like a miniature sun in the midst of multiple nets. With a *poof!* the nets burst, collapsing in on themselves and fading. When the glow disappeared, the grenade fell in on itself, the explosives spent and the shrapnel contained.

"What the hell?" came the man's voice. "Dud?"

"Or she somehow stopped it," the woman said, a whole lot more cautious than he was.

Ten seconds, Wolfe warned. *Pushing the metal fragments out now.*

I looked at my hand, and sure enough, there was a tiny sliver of metal emerging from my skin like it was being born from my flesh. One dropped out of my forehead like a shadowy, miniature suicide jumper plummeting out of my skull. My kidney felt better, my heart didn't hurt like death anymore; I was down to a mild ache in my chest and the thousand angry hornet stings around my body from the grenade shrapnel felt like nothing worse than needle pricks. I still felt like Hellraiser, but I sat up, blood and dew brushing off in the grass, leaving a bed of dark stains in the dirt.

I need to move, I said, and Gavrikov obliged. Whisper quiet, I surged further into the darkness of the grassy area between the bar's parking lot and the business next door. I swooped around the corner of the fence, and out of sight before my attackers could turn the corner and catch sight of me.

Behind the bar, the fence wrapped the building, wood and impenetrable. That was fine; it gave me cover as I came around it at a hundred miles an hour. I looped the building quick, figuring I'd get the drop on whoever had attacked me, make them pay for not finishing the job.

The only thing I was undecided on was how badly I'd make them pay.

Death, Wolfe whispered.

There can be only one sentence for this crime, Bjorn agreed.

The government is not going to protect you, Bastian said. *They've as good as declared open season on you. Maybe it's time to let everybody know that open season on Sienna Nealon means open season FOR Sienna Nealon.*

If they will not protect you with the rule of their law, why adhere to their law? Gavrikov asked.

No one in this city is looking out for you, Eve said. *No one here will stop them from killing you. It's not their job. And even the ones who don't want them to kill you aren't going to interfere.*

Zack? I asked as I came around the back of the bar. Two dark shapes were moving in the night, creeping around the fence where I'd gone, taking their time. One of them was most definitely female, and she was holding a big rifle. Looked like an M-14, complete with a nice scope.

I don't know. Zack sounded torn. *They're right, no one's going to protect you but you ... but ...*

But what? I asked, hovering, just at the corner, waiting. I was so torn up, so empty inside, so wounded ... I didn't trust my own judgment. My instincts were to torch them from a distance, burn both of them alive by heating their blood to five thousand degrees and just letting them cook here in the parking lot, two less killers in the world to worry about.

Killing them and embracing the image of you that they're putting out there ... it feels like giving up, he said. *Like giving in and saying, Yep, Sienna Nealon is the murderer you all think she was.* He was quiet when next he spoke. *You're not a quitter, Sienna. And yeah, it's bad right now. I can't promise it's going to get better anytime soon, but ... if you do this ... I can promise it will never get better. Never.*

I unclenched my fist. *They don't want me to even defend myself. They don't respect me. They want me to lie down and die. They'll hate me until I'm a victim, and maybe even then.*

I know, Zack said. *It's unfair.*

It's bullshit! Gavrikov said. *It should be the sovereign right of every person to fight back if someone means to kill them.*

What message does this send? Eve asked. *That we should lie down and die for our attackers?*

That we should measure our response, Zack said.

Try measuring a response in a life or death situation, Wolfe said. *It's the quickest way to die.*

In a fight, Bastian said, *you take your enemies out. I don't care who you are. She didn't go looking for this, but you can't expect her to just sit there and dilly while people are shooting her through the heart. That's insane.*

But she's still alive now, Zack said. *She doesn't have to kill them. Not here. Not now. She can take them out, no problem, without killing them.*

Fine, this time, Eve said. *But she has already taken them out, shown them mercy once. How many times must she turn her back on them before they kill her? Because they very nearly did this time.*

I don't know, Zack said.

What if they get out again? Bjorn asked. *They were turned loose once, what's to stop it happening once more? And next time they finish the job, for they will never underestimate her again.*

I don't have an answer for that, Zack said.

No, you have an answer, Eve snarled, *and your answer seems to be mercy, mercy unto her death.*

This affects me, too, you know, Zack said.

No, it doesn't, Eve said. *It doesn't affect any of us, really. We're passengers. When she hurts, we don't really feel it. If she dies, our consciousness get snuffed out for the final time, this hollow remnant of our existence swept off the mortal coil, but it's her who will die, you idiot. You have no skin in the game, no flesh on the line. You are like one of those politicians making their calculation at a distance, consoling yourself by saying, "You have to break a few eggs to make an omelet," while overlooking that it's not your eggs that are being broken, and the peoples' whose it is aren't getting the damned omelet.* I could almost feel her passionate intensity as she turned her attention on me. *Sienna, there is no love lost between us, but Ariadne loves you as she would a daughter. Your life is on the line, and these people, the moment they got out of prison with a fresh start, threw it away to hunt and kill you. They will not stop. They will not be gently rehabilitated. They will kill you if they can, and this soft-minded idiot would give them every opportunity. Do not be a fool. End them now.*

"I don't think I can do that," I whispered.

Then be it on your head, Eve said, *when their next shot hits you in the brain. I won't shed any tears, though I hurt for the one who will.* And she disappeared into the recesses of my mind.

"I need help," I said, lingering behind the corner of the fence. "Non-lethal."

Let us break their minds, Bjorn said.

You're with me? I asked.

I could almost see Bjorn grin in the dark, like a Cheshire cat's teeth showing in the corner of my vision. *I would not back from a fight.*

I stand with you, Gavrikov said. *Foolhardy though this decision is, I suppose it is admirable.*

You choose odd ground on which to make your moral stand, Wolfe said. *Didn't you drown a woman in her own vault just a few months ago?*

That was different, I said. *Others were at risk, there was no recourse. These people ... we can take them down. They will go to jail. And if they don't ...*

They will, Zack said. *You can't kill them ... but Scott didn't say you had to lie down and die. Just fight back, subdue them. They'll be back in the Cube, and this time they'll stay there.*

"Let's do this," I said, and swept toward them.

I flew across the parking lot, low over a parked car, and when I was twenty feet away, I said, *Bjorn, now.*

The woman screamed and dropped her rifle, the heavy stock rattling hard against the parking lot pavement as it dropped. It fired into the air, sending a shot off, and I came down on her, kicking her through the fence. It shattered rotted planks and she kept going, slamming into the side of the building next door.

The man peeked his face around the corner of the busted fence, and his teeth glinted in the light of the lamp post. "Shafer," I muttered and leapt toward him. He was an Iron Tooth, and that meant his mouth was pretty much invulnerable to conventional punching, so I went low and hit him right in the sternum instead.

Bones cracked, and he gasped, air leaving him. I pounded his ribs a few times with each of my fists, breaking my own hands and letting them knit back in the process. *Keep it up, Wolfe.*

Can we—

"No," I said, and hit Shafer so hard that he started to go airborne as well. I grabbed his belt and yanked on it, ripping it free and depriving him of the two grenades he still had on it, as well as his pistol. I tossed them back toward Borosky's—his girlfriend's—rifle, and heard it all clank as it hit the pavement in the parking lot.

I zoomed over to them as Borosky was starting to get up and dealt her a punch to the face that knocked her cold. Her eyes rolled back in her head and she went slack. Police sirens wailed in the distance, and Shafer was just getting to his feet, clutching his ribs, when I heard one turn onto the street.

I didn't have much time, so I rocketed over to him, grabbed him by the forehead, and said, "Night night." I rammed his skull into the asphalt, shattering pavement and causing his eyelids to flutter and close.

"Take that," I said weakly, not feeling much of anything but tired. I was a bloody and tattered mess, but I'd beaten them. Beaten them and their backstabbing sneak attack. "You bastards. I'm not quitting. I'm not going down that easy … Harmon." I said it even though he wasn't there, wasn't listening. It was almost like a prayer, like I hoped he could hear me.

Like I hoped he would know I wasn't going to make it easy on him.

I stood over both of them, Borosky and Shafer, hands in the air. I figured I'd make it easy on the cops, though, and I did, just standing there, in surrender to the law, waiting for the police to pull in and sort this whole mess out.

31.

"I want to press charges," I said for the hundredth time. Lights were flashing all around me, again, and I was tired of this scene. Tired of being surrounded by cops, by fire trucks, by ambulances. I wanted to go home but I didn't have a home anymore. I wanted to be anywhere but here, yet I was stuck here, watching over Borosky and Shafer while the Bloomington PD administered the suppressant drugs that had made their way into usage among every major police department in America.

"Yes, ma'am," an officer named Gustafson said. He was a pretty cool dude, and by cool I mean unflappable. His lips had been a straight line the entire time I'd known him— about half an hour now—that told me he was neither impressed with me nor that excited to be in my presence. It could have been worse, though; at least he was being professional about it, and he wasn't actively running away from me.

"Sorry," I said, apologizing reflexively. Shafer wasn't awake, but Borosky had regained consciousness and was blinking heavily, almost as if someone had concussed her. Hmm. "Can I take a second and talk to her?"

Gustafson cocked an eyebrow at me. "You want to talk to the woman you're pressing assault charges against?"

"Just a question," I said. "She and her boytoy are probably the dozenth people to come after me in the last two days. I have a feeling this is all coming from somewhere, and I just want to mention a name to her, see if she reacts."

Gustafson looked over his shoulder at where another cop was trying to get Borosky up off the curb where they'd cuffed her. "I don't think she's going to be much good at answering anything right now."

"Can I try? Pretty please?"

"Since you asked so nice," Gustafson said, looking completely unimpressed. He beckoned me forward and followed as I walked over to her. Borosky never once made eye contact with me, her head bobbing like she'd suffered serious neurological damage. She was a meta, so it would probably heal. Probably.

"Rosanna?" I asked, and she blinked and bobbed her head while lifting it up to look at me. "Where's Cassidy?"

Borosky blinked at me, trying to concentrate. "Huh?"

"Where's Cassidy Ellis?" I asked. "The woman who hired you?"

"I don't … are you Cassidy?" Borosky looked at me blankly.

"I don't think she knows who you're talking about," Gustafson said. Astute guy. He was either right, and she was clueless, or she was the world's best liar. I was prepared to accept a third option, though—I'd dinged her brain so hard that she'd honestly forgotten who Cassidy was and why she'd sent her here.

"Guess not," I said, stuffing my hands in my jeans pockets. They squished, because my pockets were filled with blood that had yet to dry. Cold blood that had dripped down from all my various wounds. I yanked my hands out of my pockets, once more covered in red streaks. The sad thing was, I'd done this about five times now.

"Who's this Cassidy person?" Gustafson asked. Dude still looked like he either didn't know where he was or just didn't care.

"Another of the Cube detainees that got out a few days ago," I said. "We called her the Brain, because she had beyond-genius-level-IQ. Dumb as a post when it came to figuring out human nature, though."

"Got a captain like that," Gustafson grunted.

I turned back to Borosky. "Hey, Rosanna," and she

163

bobbed her head, trying to focus on me, "how'd you find me?"

Borosky stared at me, still bobbing, unable to keep her eyes locked on me. I was about to write her off as a hopeless case when she burbled, "Tracked your cell phone."

I blinked. I damned sure hadn't expected a truthful answer. I pulled it out of my pocket and stared at the little lump of plastic and metal. Suddenly it made sense why she and Shafer had bushwhacked me outside a bar where I'd stopped on a whim, without telling a soul I was going to do it. "How'd you know how to do that?" I asked.

She stared at me, as best she could with the bobbing head that she couldn't hold up straight. "We're assassins, duh. Finding the people we want to kill is what we do."

"Holy hell," Gustafson said, and his mouth was slightly agape. "Did we Miranda her yet?" The officer at her side nodded. "Whew. That sounded like an admission of guilt to me."

"Yeah," I said, "a real open and shut case."

"Ye—" Gustafson started to say, but another pair sirens—everyone else had switched theirs off—broke through the night and split the quiet buzz of conversation around the crime scene as a black SUV pulled up just outside the yellow tape perimeter. "What's this?"

"Feds," I said, thrusting my hands into my pockets again and rolling my eyes as they squished in my own blood once more. It wasn't even close to drying; there was just too much of it, like I'd washed my clothes in my own gore.

Scott popped out of the SUV a second later, and Friday got out right behind him. I was sick of seeing the two of them but I held in my nausea, as they sauntered over to me—well, to Gustafson, because they ignored the hell out of me—and Scott asked, "Are you the officer in charge of the scene?"

"That's me," Gustafson said, and somehow his straight-line of a mouth got even straighter than when he'd been dealing with me. "You are?"

"FBI." Scott flashed his ID. Friday just lurked with his arms folded, swelled once more to beyond normal size.

"What's the story?"

"Attempted murder," Gustafson said. I didn't mind him answering for me. Anything to keep me from having to say bupkis to these assclowns was fine by me. "The lady took a shot at Ms. Nealon here, the gentlemen tossed grenades at her. The woman admitted to tracking her by cell phone, and they ambushed her as she came out of the bar."

"And yet she's not dead," Scott said, clearly unimpressed. He gave me a once over.

"No, I'm totally fine," I said, "except for all this blood, y'see. Got shot through the heart, and the kidney, took a hundred or so pieces of grenade shrapnel I had to heal from."

"Your mouth still works fine, I see," Scott said.

"So does hers." I tossed a thumb over my shoulder to indicate Borosky. "She copped to tracking me. You've got a mountain of physical evidence from the gun to the bullets, so ..." I threw my hands wide. "Congrats."

Scott ignored me, looking everything over with a detached calm. He did this for a few seconds, making my stomach tangle into knots, and then, finally, when he'd given it serious thought, he turned to Gustafson and said, "Cut 'em loose."

That landed like a bomb, provoking a stunned silence. "Sir," Gustafson said, politely, Minnesota Nice forcing a strange *Are you serious?* smile onto his face for the first time since I'd met him, "they used firearms and explosives in a public place—"

"Did you see it?" Scott asked, honing in on him. His face was so flat, so expressionless, that he would have won a contest with the Gustafson of thirty seconds earlier, and that was saying something.

"No, sir," Gustafson said, leaning hard on his manners in a way that suggested to me he was trying to keep some emotion from coming out, "but Ms. Nealon—"

"Ms. Nealon," Scott cut right over him as I stood there, speechless, retreating into myself by the second, "is untrustworthy and would be torn apart on any witness stand, in any court of law. Let them go."

Gustafson stood there for a long moment, and when he

spoke, it felt like a gunshot in the quiet. "But they tried to kill her." I looked at him again, and gone was the passive, plain, restrained demeanor. He was staring at Scott in flat disbelief, like he was trying to determine if he'd heard him right.

"Says her," Scott said, unwavering. "Says a serial liar and murderer." He didn't even look at me as he said any of this. "I'm not going to repeat myself—they are not going to the Cube, and if you try and stick them in your local jail, the Department of Justice is going to come at you." He took a step closer to Gustafson, whose expression was starting to harden, probably because he could sense he was being threatened.

"Come at me for what?" Gustafson asked, exuding defiance.

Scott paused to grin before answering, and it was just as horrible as when he'd smiled when he kept me from stopping my house burning down. "Anything. Everything at our disposal—lawsuits, turning the press loose on you, putting you under the microscope. Your life will be hell, and anything you do to try and keep them in will be for nothing, because sooner or later … they'll get out."

Gustafson just stared at him, like he was trying to decide how to respond, but as he opened his mouth to do so, I spoke first. "You asshole," I said to Scott.

Scott looked at me coldly. "What's that?"

"He'll do it," I said to Gustafson, who was frozen with his own mouth open, an intemperate response about to leak out. "He'll wreck you for trying to hold them, and it'll all be for nothing. Just …" I closed my eyes. "Just let them go. Save yourself the hell." I opened my eyes again.

Gustafson stared at me, and his lips were pursed. Still in a line, but pursed. "I'm sorry, ma'am," he finally said. "Before we let them loose, maybe you should—"

"I want to question her," Scott said.

"For what?" Gustafson got up in his face. "You already said there's no crime here. So what do you need to question her for?"

Scott's ruddy face lost a shade or two of complexion. "Watch yourself, officer." He gave it a moment's thought.

"Fine. She can go." He looked right at me. "For now."

"Thanks," I said and leapt past him, missing him by less than an inch. Friday swept out a hand, trying to knock me off course, but he was too slow, and I dodged around it, hurtling off once more in the only way I could, leaping away from the crime scene before they could turn the two people loose who had just tried to murder me before they could get a third chance.

32.

I stopped briefly in east Bloomington to smash my phone to pieces without fully considering the consequences. I'd had this one for a while without destroying it; I guess it only made sense that Borosky and Shafer could track it. I'd certainly tracked suspects by their cell phones in the past; I just hadn't reckoned someone would turn that around on me.

Unfortunately, that move cut me off from being able to call any of the people I usually relied on for support. I hadn't talked to Reed in what felt like forever, though in reality it had only been a day. He was probably almost fully recovered by now, but I couldn't know for sure because I'd just destroyed my lifeline.

I could pick up another tomorrow from my office, if I wanted to risk going there. I could pick one up at a phone store as well. I was lucky my contacts were stored in the cloud, because I'd be damned if I could remember anyone's number.

I came down after another giant leap, this one carrying me over the sparsely trafficked interstate 494. I landed outside a hotel, walked quickly under the portico and into the front door. It was the middle of the damned night, and there was a lady in a professional-looking business suit behind the front desk. She glanced up as I entered and smiled. "Welcome! You looking for a room for the night?"

"Boy, am I," I said, and as I got closer to her, she stared at my clothing. I had already forgotten I was covered in blood.

She shrugged after a minute, apparently writing it off as part of the shirt's design or something, and tapped away at the keyboard in front of her.

"King room or a double?" she asked.

"King."

"All right," she kept up the pleasant demeanor. "How many nights will you be staying with us?"

"At least one," I said. "Can I leave it open-ended for now?"

"Sure," she said, not looking up from the keyboard until she finished a final few taps. "I'll need a credit or debit card and your ID, Ms …?"

"Nealon." I pulled both out of my back pocket and put them on the counter in front of her.

She stared at my ID for a long second, and then took a stumbling step back from the counter, her smile gone. She looked at me like I was diseased, like she wanted nothing more than to have the ability to fly just so she could soar away from me, zip out the back and never see me again. "No," she said.

My mouth fell open. "'No' what?"

"No," she said, shaking her head. "Just no. We don't need this." She shook her head harder. "We don't need … you … here."

I felt like she'd slapped me across the face rather than backpedaled from me as quickly as humanly possible. I blinked a few times, stunned, feeling cold inside, and picked up my ID and credit card. Without another word, I walked back out into the cold night.

I couldn't recall ever feeling quite so rejected. She'd acted like I was a carrier of the plague, like what I had was so awful and contagious that she couldn't bear to be in the same building with me, and I'd taken it without pushing back.

Then again, what was the point of pushing back? She was a night manager of a hotel, and I was the most powerful human being in the world. I could smear her all over her desk area like she was a fly that buzzed me, and she knew it. It was probably why she was so scared and revolted at the very sight of me. People had reacted strangely to me for a long while, some of them even pretty nasty about it. I'd been spat on, cold-shouldered, gotten a million awkward stares and more than a few leers.

But this … this was new.

I didn't even make it to the front desk at the next hotel. The clerk's eyes got wide and he said, "Please don't hurt me!" before running out of the room and leaving me alone in the lobby.

In the third hotel I found myself served by a guy with the least amount of give-a-shit of anyone I'd ever met, a slacker to the max, and I was so grateful when he took my credit card and my ID without comment that I almost wanted to kiss him. Except that I probably would have been so enthusiastic it would have lasted too long, and then he would have died and I would have had slacker soul in my head forevermore. He was better admired from a distance, I decided.

I made it up to my room without encountering another human being, and as soon as I was in, I shed my bloody clothing. There was nothing for it; I didn't have new clothes. I thought about visiting a Wal-Mart, because there was one nearby, but I couldn't bring myself to face the world yet, even though I knew that the middle of the night would be the best time to get new clothes. If I waited until tomorrow, I was almost guaranteed to have to face more people, and that sounded like a losing formula to me.

Still, I couldn't motivate myself to get out the door.

I showered and collapsed on the bed, warring with myself. I was tired, but I needed new clothes. I was tired, but I didn't know if I could sleep. I was tired, but part of me wanted to turn on the cable news nets and see what kind of shit they were talking about me.

I didn't motivate myself to get up, and I didn't dare close my eyes, but I did manage to turn on the TV to cable news, thus proving that when faced with a decision, I did occasionally pick the very worst one possible for myself. At least shopping for clothes or sleeping would have had some positive result if I'd managed to pull them off. Watching cable news was like deciding to self-harm my psyche.

It only took ten seconds for me to figure out that, yes, 90% of news coverage was about me. They were set up with a live feed, again, in front of my office, where the reporter on scene was breathlessly (why are these people always breathless? Do they not do cardio?) telling me and the other five viewers awake at this hour that there had been an incident in Bloomington earlier tonight that was being attributed to me. They didn't have anyone live at that scene, fortunately, because really, that bar was a shithole, and I needed to associate my sagging reputation with it like I needed another hole in my heart.

I lay on the soft bed, naked because I had nothing to wear that wasn't covered in blood, and tried to remember the last time I'd felt this lonely. It took a while, because in spite of the other hell I'd faced in the last year or so, I'd felt somewhat warm and insulated from the nasty arrows of life for a while now. I thought back, back to when I'd last been alone, really alone, and realized it was just before I met Augustus. I was living at the agency, Reed wasn't talking to me, and Kat had just sold me out on national television.

"It's been a year," I whispered to myself. "Over a year."

That had felt like dark times, too. But I'd come through it, obviously. Reed and I had patched things up, Augustus had helped lighten the load. Even Kat had come back and we'd made peace. She was even trying to figure out how to help my public image. Ariadne was living with me like a den mom ...

"I haven't been alone—really alone—for the past year ... until now," I said to the quiet room. The bedspread felt rough against my back, scratchy like I was lying in a bed of thorns.

Now I was alone again, and I could feel it. I missed my phone, and suddenly felt a dash of remorse at ignoring Ariadne's calls earlier. That was stupid. Ariadne was always full of encouragement, and usually when I needed it most.

And now ... I definitely needed it.

I closed my eyes and listened to the steady stream of stupid flowing out of the reporter's mouth. At least her voice was soothing. I was dazed, dozing, and quite content to drift off, when a voice broke through the haze that wasn't soothing.

"… Seems like everywhere she goes," the man said in a lazy drawl, "people get hurt." My eyes snapped open and I focused on the screen. There was a broad, sneering face on it, one that looked a little weird without being composed of metal. "I mean this is her office," Clyde Clary, Jr. said, pointing over his shoulder at the building behind him. He really was outside my damned office. They had turned the son of a bitch loose, and I could see other members of his damned family in the background, along with Thunder Hayes, Bronson McCartney and Louis Terry, all loitering. "People'll probably get hurt here, too, before the night is over," he said, and laughed, looking right at the camera.

My hotel room suddenly lost all warmth. The reporter plowed right past his last statement, apparently seeing nothing wrong in what he'd said. I'd caught it, though, probably because I knew him, and knew what kind of violent beasts the Clarys were.

He had just threatened everyone around my office building. All those reporters on scene, looking for a story, and they'd just missed a big, honking, obvious one.

Someone had just given an interview in which he threatened to kill them all.

Just so he and his family could draw me out to the one place I had left to go.

33.

"I could just leave," I said to the empty room. "Just … fly away. The FAA can't really detect me on their radar, especially if I stay low." The heater was humming in the corner, throwing off enough warm air that the shivering I was doing was because of the emotions I was feeling about the choices open to me, not because of the air temperature on my naked skin. "I could be in California before sunrise, hunkering down with Reed and the others." I put my hands on my arms and rubbed the bare flesh. Little goosebumps had popped up on my skin.

That's not you, Sienna, Zack said softly. *You can't leave those reporters to—*

Death and blood? Wolfe asked. *Sure she can. It would be easy, and deserved.*

They have done nothing but attack her, Bjorn said with haughty self-satisfaction.

They hate her, Gavrikov said.

Going to bat for your avowed enemies may sound noble, Bastian said, *but it's actually stupid.*

They won't change their minds about her, Eve said, slinking out of the darkness to rejoin the conversation. *Nothing will. They won't even see her coming as meant to save them. They'll say she came to pick on the poor, stupid Clarys, who wanted nothing but peace.*

That's … really cynical, Zack said.

"It might not be wrong, though," I said, shivering again. I could almost see Eve nodding at my approbation in the dark spaces of my mind. "Clearly no one picked up that Junior was threatening the people around the building."

Maybe he wasn't, Wolfe said. *Maybe he was just trying to lure you so he and his family of tough meat could try and slaughter you again.*

"I've been fighting that family for years," I said. "They're dumb, but direct. The moment they got out they were guaranteed to beeline for me—which in this case, meant my office, since my house is ashes. Hell, they might have even done that, depending on when they got out." I shivered again, and ran fingers through my hair. There was still dirt stuck in there from when I'd taken my dive in the dewy grass. "If it was Junior fishing for me, I'd be surprised."

You think he'd really kill innocent reporters— Zack started

There is no such thing as innocent reporter, Bastian said with a little heat.

But there is such a thing as a tasty one, Wolfe said with a grin.

"Gross," I said, breezing past another cannibalism reference, and I settled into the silence. "I *could* just leave," I said again. It felt like I was battling to convince myself, trying to push myself to fight the instincts, to just run. They wouldn't really hurt reporters, would they? They were pissed at me and all, but killing innocent people on the off chance I'd come running?

It's the Clary family, Zack said. *They're not overly bright, and they don't care who they hurt.*

They don't even really care if they go to jail, Eve added.

You assume any conventional police force or FBI task force could get them to go to jail, Bastian said. *I have my doubts that your ex the Waterboy or his gal Friday have the muscle to put down two stoneskins in steel form. All the suppressant in the world doesn't do you any good if you can't get them to take a breath of it or punch through the skin to administer it.*

I froze in my pacing and shivered yet again. The bumps on my arms were like tiny molehills sticking out on my pale skin. "Dammit," I whispered. "They might do nothing, though. They might just sit there all night and—"

Get angrier and angrier, Eve said. *Like Clarys do. Limited intellect and capacity to understand are the hallmarks of these morons. You killed the brains of their operation, because the mother was the only*

one who seemed to have enough of a mind to keep the others from getting their heads stuck in a boot.

"Oh, hell," I muttered, putting a hand to my forehead. Ma had kept them at least somewhat disciplined in their approach. From what I'd seen of Junior he was a chip off the ol' blockhead, without much in the way of a brake on his emotional appetites. "If they go nuts in a crowd of reporters—"

It will definitely be Must-See TV, Wolfe said.

I would watch that over and over, Bjorn agreed.

"You … people … are … sick!" I yelled, and spun around again, pacing back in front of the bathroom door. I shot a look at the TV for the millionth time since Junior had made his little admission that no one else had caught. There was no sign of violence, but the Clarys were still there in the background with the other Three Stooges, Terry, McCartney and Hayes. "I count seven of them and one of me."

Bombard them from above and be done with it if you must intervene, Gavrikov said.

Nuke them from orbit? Zack asked. *Seriously?*

It's the only way to be sure, Bastian quoted with glib amusement.

"Doubt that's going to improve my standing," I said. "Or keep me out of jail."

Then what the hell are you going to do? Zack asked. *Strut in like you own the place and hope they throw the first punch?*

I sighed, and looked into the open bathroom, where my bloody clothes were waiting, strewn over the bathtub's edge, dripping red on the tile. "It is my office," I said, coming to a grudging decision. It wasn't the one I wanted to make, but it was the one I had to make. "And if I walk in and they attack me … then we've got our answer, and a justification for fighting back."

There was a long pause as the voices in my head shut up and digested that. Wolfe spoke first. *And if they kill you before you can retaliate?*

"Then I guess my problems will be over," I said, stepping into the bathroom and flipping the switch. It was time to suit up, and in this case my suit was my clothes, drenched in my own blood and probably quite cold. I couldn't stop shivering as I pulled them back on, the only part of me that was still warm was my cheeks, the teardrops rolling down as I dressed in silence to go out to meet my fate.

34.

I came leaping down about a hundred yards away from my office building, and the scene, which I could hear even at a distance, went pin-drop quiet in an instant. The night was dark, the gleam of a hundred nearby lamps and lights holding the black sky at bay. Reporters with spotlights shone in their eyes looked up from their live reports, dazed at the sound of my feet thumping against the pavement as I landed.

The silence held for only a second, and then the shouted questions started:

"Ms. Nealon, how do you respond to the allegations that you were involved in an assault in Bloomington this evening?"

"What do you plan to do now?"

"Sienna, who designed the look you're sporting tonight?"

Who the hell *was* that idiot?

I ignored the questions, using Gavrikov's power to elevate me a couple feet off the ground. Most people who saw me on TV were always left with the illusion that I was taller than I actually was. In this case, I wanted the height because at 5'4", there was no way I could keep an eye on the Clarys or Thunder Hayes's contingent of troublemakers through the crowd of reporters that mobbed me as I approached.

The whole Clary family was watching me, just watching, from about thirty feet away. They were staring at me with surly, sullen gazes, Hayes and his crew clumped together with them like old fraternity buddies. The Brotherhood of Sienna-Kicked-My-Ass, surely. They didn't do anything more

177

than watch, though, as I made my way through the crowd toward the front doors.

"Excuse me," I said, keeping my voice low and polite. If the Clarys didn't start anything, I damned sure wasn't. I would just go in, try and find one of the spare cell phones that J.J. kept on hand for me in case of my inevitable destruction of my current one, and saunter back out.

Easy as pie.

"Please," I said to the reporters shoving cameras in my face as I kept my gaze anchored on my enemies across the crowd. "Excuse me."

"Sienna!"

"Ms. Nealon!"

"How do you respond to the allegations—"

"Who does your hair, Sienna?"

I didn't answer anyone, especially that last jackass, just kept making my way through, slowly but surely. The Clarys and their crew started to move, edging toward the front door to my office. I took a deep breath and watched them out of my peripheral vision. They were too big to miss, so there wasn't much point in turning this into a staring contest. They were taking it real easy, too, not shoving or elbowing their way over. They just slowly eased until they were standing close to the door, lined up along my parade route, waiting for me.

I made it through the crowd of reporters and someone bonked me on the head with a boom microphone. They didn't apologize, but it didn't hurt, so I just ignored it, rubbing my head where it had hit. I could feel the crowd around me, their chatter overwhelming my meta senses, the strange sensation of all of them just there, inches away, like I could still feel them even if I closed my eyes, blocked my ears and held my hands close to my chest.

I didn't stare directly at the Clarys. I just kept walking, set to pass right in front of them. I took it nice and slow, waiting for them to say something.

"So they already let you guys out of Arkham, huh?" I asked as I went by.

"Looks like someone did a number on you, bitch," Janice

Clary said, spitting at my feet. I'd remembered her name once I was sober. She didn't even bother to take a shot at me.

"Cool it," Junior whispered. "You are looking a little worn, girl. Someone got a bite out of you, huh?"

"More than a bite," McCartney pronounced, hulking, his massive frame overshadowing me even now that I was walking a couple feet up in the air. "That's a lot of blood." All of them were talking at such a low, meta-only volume that there was no chance even a press mic would have picked them up over the crowd noise.

"Good," Denise Clary sneered without letting her face get too sour. They had apparently been coached for the camera, because they were really holding it in.

I paused, and looked over at them, keeping my demeanor calm, even sad. I could play this game, too. "Where's Cassidy?"

A wave of visible discomfort ran through them, and stares were exchanged. "Whatchoo talking about?" Louis Terry said awkwardly.

"Never mind," I said, and went for the door, taking slow paces, waiting for one of them to open up on me.

No one did.

Once I was inside, I hurried to J.J.'s office. I only hoped McCartney had overlooked something in his haste to trash the place. It didn't take me long to find the spare cell phones, hidden in a box in the bottom drawer of J.J.'s desk. It didn't really look like anything special, though, so while McCartney had overturned the desk, the phones within were just fine.

I couldn't chance carrying the box out, for fear that having something that big in my arms would interfere with my ability to fight, so I activated one and waited for it to boot up while I stuck two more in my pockets. That was a primary, a secondary, and a final backup, and it emptied the box of spares. I'd need to be careful with them; this was likely the last time I'd be able to get my hands on any until I got to California and hit up a cell phone store.

I debated waiting for the phone I'd picked as my new primary to sync and decided against it. I'd walked past the

Clary gauntlet and waited to see who'd hit me with it. They'd passed, at least on the first round. They were being remarkably restrained, which suggested to me that they had no intention of starting shit that would get them in trouble. That suggested something further, in fact, which had been revealed with their discomfort at a single question.

Cassidy was running this show. And whatever she'd said to them, it had them fearful enough that they'd mended fences with her and were now taking her orders. Orders which appeared to extend as far as not starting a war with me in full view of the media. Oh, they'd fight one with me, for sure, but apparently they didn't want to be seen as the aggressors. It made sense, really, because half the hell Cassidy had put me through last time had been turning the press against me so viciously that I'd begun to wonder if anyone out there in the world didn't hate me.

All I had to do to walk out of this … was to walk out of it. The press would still hate me, my enemies would still be lurking out there. But I wouldn't have to fight them to the death, at least not today, and not here, at this place of their choosing.

And not alone.

I held the phone in my hand as the little bar indicating that it was loading continued to scroll across. I needed to get to California, needed to get back to my friends, to the only family I had left. Dealing with this in isolation, alone, was a terrible strategy. Nothing had gone my way since I'd chosen to stay here and fight on the ground my enemies had chosen for me. I'd barely escaped death, and if I stayed here, waiting for them to come at me again, I'd be lucky if I survived the week.

I pocketed the last phone, and turned. Part of me wanted to sneak out the back, or head up to the roof and fly away into the darkness. But I couldn't get Clyde Jr.'s seeming threat out of my head.

They let you pass, Wolfe said. *You've done enough.*

This is plenty of danger for any sane person to expose herself to, Bjorn said. I liked how he included me in the ranks of the sane.

"I need to be sure," I said, taking a deep breath. I could hear the crowd outside, reporters filing their on-scene reports about how I'd just walked through to my office in the middle of the night. I imagined the Clarys wading through them with steel fists, pulping skulls and leaving blood on the pavement.

I couldn't walk away from that without being sure.

My phone buzzed in my hand, already set to vibrate, and I slid it to unlock. There were a few voicemail notifications, but I didn't want to check those, not yet. One popped up: *Kat Forrest has shared her location with you.* I clicked it, and it brought up a map of North America that zoomed slowly in to the San Francisco Bay area. It closed on a suburb east of the city, and finally on a house, popping up a little balloon with an address that I repeated to myself six times, just to be sure I had it. Just in case something happened to my phone.

"This is it," I whispered to myself. I took a few deep breaths, in and out, and then walked out of the office, into the waiting chill of the autumn night.

35.

The noise level outside exploded once again as I stepped out. The Clary family was glaring at me, their backs to the media scrum so none of the watching cameras could see them give me the stink eye. Clearly the press thought nothing of them being here. I couldn't decide whether that was because they were hoping to see a brawl break out, or if they really just didn't think anything of them being here, in spite of my arrest of them in the past. It was hard to tell whether they were just so negligent they didn't know these people had been prisoners at the Cube, or if they didn't care. Maybe they thought they were all innocent victims of my authoritarian ways.

Whatever the case, the Clarys and Hayes and his boys all stood in a line as I came out the door. I looked at them warily as I walked past, keeping my hands at my sides. All it would take would be one of them reaching for a gun and I'd be legally justified to pull Shadow and start emptying the magazine at anyone who came at me in a threatening manner. I still had the gun riding at my back, but I was scared to pull it for anything less than certain death coming my way. I felt pretty confident that if I used my weapon in anything less than a scenario where my death was assured, I'd be crucified for it.

"See ya later, guys," I said amiably to the whole line of scowling faces as I went past, taking particular care not to infringe on their personal space. Denise Clary started to step out at me, but Junior caught her by the shoulder, and she stopped.

"Yeah, you will," Junior said. "We ain't gonna forget what you done to our momma."

"Or our daddy," Buck Clary said.

"You're talking about the same person, right?" I asked, playing innocent. "I mean, it was Iowa, so ... I assume they were the same person."

"Always got a smart answer for everything," Thunder Hayes said. He didn't look nearly as amused as he had the last few days when he'd been taunting me.

"I leave the dumb answers to you," I shot back, walking on past. Three of the Clarys were out of my peripheral vision now, and any one of them could have stepped right up and decked me from behind. A good, solid hit would probably even kill me. I took a breath and kept moving, listening as hard as I could, waiting for a tingle across my scalp that might warn me someone was coming at me from behind.

"Counting on the cameras to save you, Nealon?" A voice came from my left, and I turned to see a ruggedly handsome man standing there, faint scar across his nose and a sneer on his face. Lorenzo Benedetti was standing there barefoot, his sleeves up. "Where is your brother?"

"Where are all your little friends?" Bronson McCartney asked. I looked right at him and realized something very chilling.

The press had stopped talking. Completely. Not one of them was saying a word.

"I approved their vacation requests, McCartney," I said. "No need to keep them in town when everything's so quiet and under control." I stared at the mass of press in front of me, wondering what the hell had suddenly gone wrong with them. There were a lot of glassy-eyed stares, like they'd been struck dumb. Not just dumb, actually. Clary dumb.

"You never did figure out my power, did you, Nealon?" Terry asked, leering at me with his freaky blond hair like a beacon in the night.

"I assume it comes out of a peroxide bottle," I said, suddenly feeling very surrounded. With a crash, every member of the press in attendance dropped their cameras and mics. Glass lenses shattered, plastic broke, and it all made a pretty dreadful sound as it came down. They looked like they were having fits or seizures. Drool slid down chins, reporters made sounds like rabid animals, rattling deep in their throats.

"I call it ferality," Terry said with a toothy grin. "Shame it doesn't seem to be working on you. I would have liked to see you crawl on all fours like a dog." I glanced at the reporters and, sure enough, they were on their hands and knees, poised like … well, like animals, mouths open, ready for a treat.

"Whatcha gonna do, Nealon?" Hayes asked, as the reporters all made a growling sound as one. It was pretty unnerving. "Not like the press didn't want to see you die, but if you kill 'em …" He cackled, and a few of the Clarys joined in, like a pack of hyenas. "Well, it probably ain't gonna help your cause none."

"Better think fast," Terry said, and with a sweep of his hand he motioned the press corps forward. They sprang, like the animals they appeared to be, gone from merely out for my blood metaphorically to being out for it in a much more literal sense.

36.

The fight or flight instinct was settled in a hot second. Terry had turned the entire cadre of reporters encamped outside my office into his personal running monkeys, and I knew I didn't want to hurt them (seriously. Mostly. Mostly, I did not want to hurt them, in spite of what they were doing to make my life hell) so I shot up twenty feet into the air.

That did not stop them.

They climbed on each other's shoulders, like a human pyramid of angry honey badgers, not giving a shit. They bit at my ankles, leapt at me, climbed and jumped, tore at each other, and in general did a much more physical version of what they did every day, fighting and stepping on each other to get to the story.

I lingered up there for only about a second, but it was a second too long. A blast of wind tilted me, flipping me over in midair. I caught myself before slamming into the second story of my office building, and threw out a hand. Lorenzo Benedetti was lurking below, readying another gust, so I blasted him in the eye with one of Eve's light nets. It anchored around his face and masked him, and then I shot one at Terry that covered both his eyes and the top of his neon blond head. Because that color was distracting.

The moment the net blindfold hit Terry, his pack of hungry reporters suddenly seemed to lose sight of me, as though I'd taken all their eyes as well. They snarled, they snorted, they tore at each other blindly, but not one of them looked at me, and it only took me a second to realize why.

Apparently, Terry was indeed the brains of their entire operation. It was a sad commentary on what I was facing, but there it was.

"Get down here and fight like a man!" Junior Clary yelled at me.

"Um, no," I said, and glared at him as I swept his posse for signs of the next attack. I was pretty sure with the press now blind and snarling uselessly, Thunder Hayes and Bronson McCartney would be joining the battle, and so I wasn't surprised to see ol' Thunder lighting up his hands with his lightning powers.

A bolt shot past me and grounded on the office tower wall as I swept away at high speed. The last thing I needed was to get jolted right now, especially given how I'd been killed by electricity once this year already. I zoomed around the building once and came back low. Hayes must have guessed at my plan, because I had to veer off as he shot loose another bolt.

Buck and Junior were stomping around now with their metal skin, all suited up for war. Denise's hair snaked out and swiped out me as I flew past, but I didn't let her get me down, either. A bolt of lightning hit her nasty locks in lieu of me, and Denise screamed below. She tossed Thunder a dirty look, but she didn't seem to be out of the fight.

I peppered them all with light nets, with mild to moderate success. I bound one of Hayes's arms to his waist, re-upped the net I'd put on Terry (that hair, it was hideous) and then came low over the press monkeys, figuring Lorenzo was just waiting to take his shot.

I wasn't disappointed; Lorenzo gusted at me as soon as he had a clear line of fire. He really let loose, too, gale-force winds that swept along the ground toward me.

Unfortunately for him, I was quite used to dodging gusts of wind from training with Reed. I know I'm biased, but Reed was a way, way better Aeolus than this guy.

I dodged above his two-fisted power gust and then dipped right back down. My fist met his jaw with terrible, bone-cracking force, and I claimed my first KO of the night. Benedetti's eyes rolled up and he dropped to the ground.

His gusts went on, though, sweeping behind me and hitting the barrel of monkeys. Reporters went flying twenty feet into the air, like a pile of leaves in an autumn wind. They came down on my assailants, still blind and biting and scratching and clawing at anything that moved.

Finally, I found a use for these media assclowns.

Then I remembered that I was nominally trying to protect them, and quickly resolved to get the feral reporters away from my conscienceless foes, who probably wouldn't share my qualms about killing them. Shit. And it had been so fun to hoist these a-holes on their own petard.

Janice Clary had shown her mysterious powers at last. Swollen up like a female bodybuilder, she was whacking the hell out of reporters that were blindly clawing at her, grabbing them and throwing them. I shot toward her and flipped at the last, smashing her with a kick to the jaw that caused her muscles to deflate from sudden, rapid-onset unconsciousness.

Two down.

A bolt of lightning raced past me, almost connecting as it caused the hairs on my head to stand up again. Thunder Hayes was ripping off lightning bolts as fast as he could charge his little cannon, and I was right in his way. It was kinda like horseshoes and hand grenades and nuclear warfare, in that all he had to do was get a bolt close enough to me and it'd bend to hit my ass. And the rest of me.

I halted as he tried to lead me with his next shot, and he grounded his attack almost harmlessly against Buck Clary's metal self. ("Ow, dammit! I can feel that!") His hand would glow as he built up a charge, apparently not quite practiced enough to just loose a bolt without warning.

I could work with that.

I froze, pretending to linger a second too long in one place, then started to move again. I did so at about half speed, counting on my reflexes and his little charge-up warning to save me. He was taking his time this round, though, aiming carefully, and I was looming in the foreground, only a couple feet off the earth, my hand glowing and ready to release a light net as soon as I was done with this dance.

Hayes unleashed the biggest burst of lightning yet, a bolt that would have easily put out 1.21 gigawatts. I shot backward as soon as he did it, grabbing the still-blind Terry by the elbow and shoving him in front of me. "Human shield!" I shouted as the bolt of lightning hit him, and he danced under the force of the electricity.

"Gosh," I said into the stunned silence that followed. Terry keeled over, but I could still hear him breathing. Lucky bastard. "I hope they don't blame me for that." And then I blasted Hayes in the face with a light net so hard that he hit one of the brick pillars out in front of my office building and stuck there, completely restrained.

"You can't beat all of us!" Junior said, striding out, all metal and face suffused with rage set in steel.

"I'm doing all right at it so far," I said. "And you guys are bleeding talent." I looked at the mess I'd already made of their little squad. "Well, I guess maybe 'talent' is the wrong word."

"Our whole team ain't even off the bench yet," Junior said with a leer.

Something about that set off a warning in my head, but once again, it was too late. I started to zip away, away from these rogues, away from trouble, and away from the cluster of reporters that seemed stunned unconscious along with their master, Terry, but a gunshot cracked over the square, and I came tumbling down, landing face-first on the asphalt about a hundred feet away from the Clary clan.

I realized as the pain started to set in that I'd landed in the middle of the street. I'd cleared the parking lot, at least, but the pain that was racking my chest was not quite as bad as what had hit me earlier, when Borosky had shot my heart. This one had probably only gotten my lung, I realized as I coughed up blood, and my chest spasmed with pain.

"Get her!" someone screamed as I started to get to my knees.

Wolfe, I said.

Working. As fast as can be done.

Someone kicked me in the face, and pain flew through me

as my jaw cracked, and teeth came loose. I caught a brief glimpse of Denise Clary crowing in triumph as she slammed her booted foot into my face.

Sienna, Gavrikov said, we need to get out of h—

I started to launch into the sky, blood running down my chin, but as I came up something grabbed me by the leg, sharp and pointed, tearing into my ankle and calf, ripping me back down. Claws tore into my back, and strong arms slammed me back into the pavement.

Bronson McCartney, form of: bear. I preferred the raccoon, honestly.

I reached for Shadow, hiding at the small of my back, and pulled it. I had almost taken aim at Thunder Hayes, who was stalking toward me, apparently free from his net bonds, when something gleamed in the night and tore into my arm. There was a flash of blood and suddenly the limb ended at the elbow, and a smiling, snarling face grinned back at me as he shook my lifeless hand and Shadow dropped into his waiting palm.

Iron Tooth Michael Shafer, all woken up from his police-induced coma.

Someone slammed a metal fist into my belly, and I felt organs rupture. A steel face, a steel hand, filled with vicious satisfaction in the form of a furious grin as he pounded on me three times in quick succession, driving the air out of my body, making me choke up blood and wonder how I could ever breathe again.

I don't think I'd ever seen Clyde Clary, Jr., look this happy. Just like his dad, he excelled in moments of cruelty, though.

"Let's finish this fast," Borosky said, walking up with her rifle in hand. *Geez, Officer Gustafson, you could have at least kept her gun.* She was pointing it at me, even though McCartney was sure to take the hit as bad as I did. "You prolong this, you give her a chance to—"

"I want to tear this bitch apart," Terry said, hobbling up to the little mob that was poised to kill me. "Gimme a second to get my hold over those—dammit." He looked over his shoulder. "They done run off. They do that, when they break free, get all spooked and go like a herd." He gave me a furious glare. "Look what you done."

I managed to get my surviving palm up, and blasted him over the head with another net before Buck Clary smashed me in the side of the head with a punch that felt like he'd beaten my skull in with a stone. I'd seen him lurking over there, but I hadn't expected him to be the one to reply. "I just wanna …" I said, blood sliding out through my swollen lips, "… cover up that … awful bottle-blond hair … is that so wrong?"

"Just do it," Borosky said coldly, and she lifted her rifle up so I could look down the barrel. McCartney's claws were still tearing at me, holding me aloft while I was dripping blood, the little half-circle surrounding me uneasy, every single one of them looking like they wanted to leap in and do the job. "Now, before she can heal again."

"She ain't healing anymore," Hayes said, and he hit me with lightning.

McCartney howled as he dropped me. "That hurt!" he said, voice muffled by his bear face.

One of the Clarys punched me into the ground. Pavement shattered, my face hit the asphalt and ricocheted back up, and I wondered how I could possibly still be alive. I couldn't feel anything below my waist.

"You're all idiots and chickenshits!" Borosky pronounced, and I heard her adjust her aim, hands rough against the wood furniture of her rifle. "Fine. I'll do it." I knew I had about a second before my skull emptied its contents all over the pavement.

But that was okay.

I didn't quit, I said to the voices in my head. I sounded weak, even to me.

You did good, Sienna, Zack said softly. I heard him swallow, and I knew the fear of what would come after that bullet blasted my brains out everywhere was filtering through him. It was coming, would be there in a second to take me away from all this. This hell.

I didn't feel it, though. The pain was starting to fade.

Death was starting to set in.

And I was done.

No, came a small voice in my ear. It was so cold, autumn chill tingling across my flesh. Except … it wasn't cold anymore … the numbness started to fade, my skin turning hot …

Not yet. The darkness around me started to fade to white, light oozing in around the edges of my vision, replacing the black that had started to claim me.

I blinked. The voice … it sounded … Russian. And like it was in my head. But there was only one Russian in my head, and his name was …

"Aleksandr Gavrikov," I murmured. The world around me exploded in a torrent of flame and heat, washing away the night and turning it to day, as an inferno was unleashed around me.

37.

I woke up and the world was on fire. I opened my eyes to a burning hellscape, in the center of a crater that seemed all too familiar for someone who had been here before. Many times. I took a breath and it was hot, the smell of brimstone and scorched earth all around me.

"Gavrikov," I whispered as I came to my feet. I was as naked as the day I was born, and the cold autumn wind whipped through once more. I shivered, and lit my skin on fire in a leotard of flame, from toes to neck, as I looked over the vista before me.

My office building was burning. The windows were shattered, and flames were leaping out of every story. The grass was gone, blackened and scorched. Cars and news vans were on fire in the parking lot, roaring in the night like bonfires in the summer.

And all around me ... stretching out from the crater where I'd awoken ...

There was nothing but two piles of molten slag that I knew had been Buck and Junior Clary. Of all the rest of my foes ... not a damned thing remained, save for a half dozen shadows scorched into the ground to mark their passage out of life.

"Gavrikov ... What have you done?" I whispered. I was still shivering, but now that my skin was on fire, it had nothing to do with the temperature.

A siren's whoop came from down the road, and I saw the black SUV coming. I knew who was in it even before it came to a screeching halt, knew who was going to get out even before Scott and Friday came piling out, Scott with a gun in his hand and a triumphant grin lit in the firelight.

"Sienna!" he shouted. "You're under arrest!"

I didn't have time to think before he fired. Four shots, at a hundred yards, and he peppered my chest. The 9mm rounds dispersed on my chest, melting to slag and falling to the earth to join the remains of the two Clarys.

I reacted without thought. Fight or flight, and this time, with the horror of what I'd just let loose, I chose flight. I soared into the sky and left Scott behind me, out of sight of him in seconds, out of the city in seconds more as I broke the sound barrier and turned west.

"What did you do, Gavrikov?" I asked, more to appease my troubled conscience that out of genuine desire to know.

The right thing, Wolfe said.

The smart thing, Bjorn said with a smirk in the darkness of my mind. I could feel the others agreeing with him, even Zack, although he seemed more reluctant than anyone else.

What I had to, Gavrikov replied at last, and with considerable more reserve than the other two had exhibited. *What I had to do in order to save your life.*

Behind me, I could see the hints of sunrise coming up in the east. I headed west and tried to outrun it, wondering how long I could hide in the dark before the light would catch me.

38.

I stopped in Sioux Falls, South Dakota, and broke into a hair salon. It sounds stupid, but I knew I needed to do it, smashing the front window and rummaging through, naked, until I found the hair dyes. I crossed town in a series of low-flying leaps, and took a page out of Terry's idiotic book and bleached my hair in an alley. Then I took the pair of clippers I stole and buzzed the sides of my scalp, leaving me with a bleached-blond mohawk.

The next step was to color what remained of my hair a psychotic shade of pink. It wouldn't have been my first choice, but when you're naked and dying your mohawk in an alley in Sioux Falls in the middle of the night, you've already failed the test for good life choices. I gave up gracefully and just got the job done, my scalp burning from the bleach in a way that reminded me of a time Michael Shafer had thrown acid on me.

When that was finished, I flew further west until I hit Rapid City. I found a clothing outlet outside town and shattered a window. I picked stuff that I would never, in a million years, wear by choice, taking care to steal enough stuff that it wouldn't look like someone—namely me—had broken in just to take one outfit. I modeled my look after J.J.'s girlfriend, Abigail, and picked up a pair of low rise jeans that were tighter around the cuff than hers, a pair of suspenders, and a tank top. I couldn't shake the feeling that I looked a little like Leeloo from *The Fifth Element*, but that was all right. I wasn't trying to blend in.

I was trying to look as different from Sienna Nealon, internationally known fugitive, as I possibly could.

The next stop was Boulder, Colorado. Now that I'd shed my flame leotard in favor of new clothes, I wasn't a naked streak in the night sky anymore. I found an all-night coffeehouse and surveilled it from across the street. I saw what I was looking for and waited a little while. It didn't take long, fortunately.

There was a hipster-looking dude wearing a hoodie and big, black-rimmed glasses just sitting in the front window, finishing his tea. I watched him until he gathered his things to leave, alone, still staring at his smartphone as he meandered off, taking a shortcut down an alleyway.

Pro tip, kids: Don't be staring at your phone when you're walking around. It makes you prey.

I came up on him from behind and slapped him in the back of the skull. Not too hard, but hard enough to make him collapse. I whacked him in the belly so he would curl up in pain, then I stole his glasses and his hoodie, and ran, not flew, off. A couple streets away, I put the hoodie on, popped the lenses out of the glasses, taking particular care to dumpster them, and put them on.

Now I'd crafted a look that practically guaranteed everyone would at least glance at me, but no one would realize who I was. The only way I could possibly have disguised myself any more effectively was if I could somehow have sprouted Wolfe's tufted beard from my cheeks and chin. But even if that were possible, it was a step too far.

I made it to California before the sun came up, scouring the suburbs of San Francisco from the sky, trying to match the darkened earth below with the map I'd seen on my phone hours earlier. Kat had sent me her location, and I'd memorized the address, but I didn't have a GPS to track it down, so I had to do it by careful study, trying to remember exactly what the place had looked like from above.

I found the right neighborhood just before sunrise, and managed to make my landing and walk the streets as the sky was turning the new color of my hair. I knew I couldn't outrun the light forever, especially given how much time I'd spent dyeing my hair and stealing clothes and stalking a hipster to steal his glasses and hoodie. It smelled funny, too, which wasn't a huge surprise given I'd gotten it in Colorado.

I walked through the neighborhood, all stucco and very Italian-villa-looking to my eyes. There was a sameness here, but the houses were large, and the lawns were medium, and I put my head down and buried my hands in my pockets and walked, looking for the address I'd memorized on that phone.

My thoughts had reached a slow bubble, days of no sleep followed by near death exertions finally taking their toll. I was cold, cold all the way to the bone, and weary, and probably paler than usual by several shades. I just wanted to find my friends, to collapse in a bed, and hope that everything that had happened tonight had been a terrible dream. I wanted to wake up in my hotel room in Bloomington and have it all turn out to be a cable-news-induced nightmare.

I turned at the right street, breathing a sigh of relief. The house numbers were steadily increasing as I wended my way up a slight hill. I didn't care that I wasn't moving at meta speed anymore. I didn't want to show myself, didn't want to reveal who I was. I just wanted to hide, to find a bed, to hug my friends, and then sleep for days. My soul felt burned, everything felt burned, as though Gavrikov had scorched off a layer of my emotions when he'd taken control and exploded.

The addresses rose and rose, and I crossed the street when I realized I was on the wrong side. A mailbox ahead proclaimed in brass, curvy numerals that I'd reached my destination, and I breathed a sigh of relief.

A sigh of relief that evaporated when I saw the front door to the house was wide open.

I stalked up the steps, breath catching in my throat. I hadn't seen Colin on my approach, blurring around, but I'd attributed that to him needing to sleep. Neither had I seen a sign of Phinneus, but I wouldn't have seen him, would I? He would have picked a vantage where he could watch unobserved.

I stepped into the darkened hallway. "Hello?" I asked. My voice sounded small in the entry, and I took a few steps in. "Is anybody here?"

I clenched my fists, my heart pounding in my ears. There was a living room just ahead, and I peered around the wall. The TV was on, but muted, and there were signs of someone having made a bed on the couch, tangled sheets that were now draped over the flowery upholstery, like it had been slept in but pushed aside for people to sit on.

I tiptoed forward, not sure why I was bothering to tiptoe. I found the kitchen, empty, but there was food laid out on the counter, a pizza half-eaten, the box open, cheese cool to the touch, grease congealed. It had broccoli on it. I put aside my disgust temporarily and moved on.

I checked the rooms; Kat's was obvious, her suitcase was undisturbed, laid out on a chest at the end of her bed, waiting for her to come in and glam herself up. Augustus's things were in a smaller bedroom, neatly piled in the corner, top of his gym bag unzipped but unmoved, as though he'd never even taken anything out of them. Ariadne's were well organized in hers, laid out for most efficient use. The room looked cleaner than the others, too, as if she'd gone over it all with a cloth when she'd arrived. I could see her doing something like that. She'd certainly cleaned up our house enough times for me to be able to picture it easily.

Reed's room had an IV line with a bag that was still half-full, the needle crusted with blood and discarded gauze pads stained red lying on the floor next to the bed. There was no sign of personal belongings in their room, probably because they didn't even have time to pack before I'd rushed them off, off to hide here ...

Here, where I didn't know what had happened to them.

J.J. and Abigail's room was unpacked, things put away in dressers and personal effects laid out on the bathroom counter. I even found Colin's room, his backpack next to an old, worn suitcase from the 1800s that looked to be Phinneus's. They were left like their owners were coming back, and I wondered if maybe they'd all snuck out in the middle of the night for an early bite.

Veronika's things were in her room, too, depriving me of my last hunch. If she'd somehow ambushed or kidnapped my friends, why leave her things behind? There was nothing of interest in her suitcase save for a half dozen of her suits, which were not cheap. She'd also left behind some pretty fancy underwear, which made me wonder what sort of use she figured she'd get out of it on this trip.

I wandered back through the house, checked the back yard, which was empty. The neighborhood was silent, and I wondered if perhaps I should search some nearby houses, see if the neighbors had noticed anything. But it was still early in the morning, I realized, and I walked back to the couch in the living room, where the TV was still going.

I felt drained, frightened, like I'd shattered myself somehow in the last few days. A cold, clammy fear had settled on me, and as I stared at the television, I felt like I was waking up from a nightmare only to find myself in a horror movie.

I couldn't escape cable news; it was on here, too, that steady flash of images between shots of reporters standing around, trying to look like they knew something. They were live in Eden Prairie, Minnesota, of course, because why wouldn't they be?

The devastation of the blast was clearer in the daylight. The ground was black, the fire finally put out in my office building. Fire hoses were still pointed at it, dumping a steady spray of water in the windows, just to be sure it didn't flare back up.

"—No one knows the whereabouts of Sienna Nealon at this hour, but local authorities have assured us that as soon as they have an accurate death toll, they will release that information to us." The reporter, a young blond lady, looked right at the camera. "As to when we'll get that number, sources say—"

"Sorry to cut you off, Glynis," the scene shifted back to another anchor, in a studio, smiling at the camera, "but we are going live now to downtown Minneapolis, where President Harmon is about to give a statement in reaction to last night's tragic events in Minnesota."

Harmon. Of course he'd show up to a scene like this. He was like a vulture sniffing a carcass—mine.

I sat down on the couch, sinking into the stuffing. I still felt cold, which was a bad sign now that I was in California. I waited, figuring Harmon would take forever to get out to the podium again, but he didn't. Apparently he was a lot happier to get out there to make his announcement this time than he had been last time, when he'd been forced to defend against my record of being a persistent pain in his ass.

"Good morning," Harmon said, not cracking a smile as he took the podium. He looked serious, his hair cut tight around his head, his eyes scanning the room in front of him as he took its temperature. "I'm going to make a very brief statement, and then turn over this press conference to our response team. Obviously, as you know, late last night into the early hours of this morning, Sienna Nealon mounted an attack on the news reporters staked out at her office." My eyes widened as I took in what he'd said. "In the process, she killed several people and also destroyed several buildings in Eden Prairie, Minnesota. This is, of course, a devastating loss to the local community as well as a terrible blow to the metahuman cause of acceptance. When I announced the arrival of metahumans on the scene five years ago, I urged caution against a rush to judgment. Throughout our history, we have made strangers of others—people we didn't understand. Our instinct is to isolate and divide ourselves from those we find dissimilar to us. I am pleased that America followed my guidance. The response to the metahuman community has been nothing but stellar, accepting and tolerant."

He paused for dramatic effect. "And in this case, entirely too tolerant. Sienna Nealon is a clear and present danger to the safety and security of the citizens of the United States of America. She is now number one on the FBI's Most Wanted list. Every state and local law enforcement agency will be receiving bulletins to be on the lookout for her. Ms. Nealon has proven herself the single most dangerous person on the face of the planet." He still didn't smile. I wondered why not;

he had to be enjoying this. "Be assured ... we will bring her to heel." He extended an arm off camera. "With that, I want to introduce the response team that will be leading this manhunt. There are some familiar faces, obviously ..."

The camera panned to Harmon's right, and my breath caught in my throat. I expected to see Scott and Friday there, and I wasn't disappointed. But the other two men standing beside them ...

If I hadn't already been sitting down, I probably would have landed on the couch hard enough to break it.

My brother, Reed, took the podium, his dark hair pulled back in a tight ponytail, Augustus only a few steps behind him. "I come before you today not as the brother of Sienna Nealon, but as the man most committed to bringing her to justice." There was no trace of sarcasm, or lies, or any of the thousand other emotions I wanted to see hidden in his brown eyes. He was serious, he was staring right into the camera, and Augustus was right behind him, doing the exact same thing. J.J. was there, too, I realized, a little off to the side. The camera angle didn't let me see anyone beyond him, but ...

... But really, that was enough to finish the job of breaking me.

"... have always backed my half-sister," Reed was saying, "but this time, she's simply gone too far. Whatever it takes, whatever measures must be used ... even lethal ones ... I will not hesitate to employ in her capture. For too long, I have stood aside and made excuses for her unconscionable behavior, have looked into the eyes of a murderer and heard her explain away her actions, hollow words from an empty soul ..."

I turned off the TV with a simple push of the remote. I sat in the quiet room, listening to a bird chirping somewhere in the distance, strangely cool.

The whole country was against me.

My enemies had come to kill me.

And now my brother and my friends had turned on me, too.

I expected to feel cold, but I'd been cold for days—out in

it, in the autumn wind, fighting against people who hated me and wanted me dead. My hand didn't shake, didn't shiver.

I stood up and walked out the front door, taking care to put my hood up. I closed the door behind me gently, so as not to wake anyone in the neighborhood with the sound of it slamming. I didn't fly off, didn't take to the skies. I started to walk back the way I came, threading my way through the neighborhood, then out onto a main street, out of the sheltered confines of suburbia, and back into a world that hated me and wanted me dead.

I was alone.

Again.

Epilogue

"Sorry I'm late," President Gerry Harmon said as he breezed into the Oval Office and plopped himself behind his desk. "Well, you know my schedule. It's been a day."

"A day I warned you would be long," Cassidy Ellis said. Harmon stared into her eyes, and knew there was so much going on behind them. "You can't back Sienna Nealon into a corner without expecting some consequences."

"I told you when we first met," Harmon said, leaning back against his chair, "I don't really care what sort of blowback comes from Sienna Nealon flailing ineffectually around. All I care about is building a better future, and if that means getting her out of the way, well, you can't make an omelet, right?"

Cassidy smiled thinly. She lacked social graces, Harmon had noticed. "Am I going to be one of those eggs?"

"You're much too valuable to be a discarded egg, Cassidy," Harmon said. He put on his most reassuring smile to do it. "You have one of the foremost minds in the world. But ..." He smiled. "Do you know your weakness?"

"People," Cassidy answered instantly.

"People," Harmon agreed. The girl was so thin he wondered if she'd break if he put a reassuring hand on her shoulder. "But, see ... I know people. And you know ... everything else. Which is why we make such a good team."

202

"But I didn't kill her," Cassidy said, flushing. "Again."

"I didn't expect you to," Harmon said, coming around the desk and resting on the edge. "I did hope that Borosky and Shafer would, but … unfortunately, even they couldn't seem to just shoot her in the head and get the job done. That's all right, though. She's pushed into the margins now. Hurting. Her own little construction of a family has turned on her."

"She's wounded," Cassidy said. "Like an animal. Don't you think that makes her dangerous?"

"Oh, almost certainly," Harmon said. "But dangerous we can deal with. And besides, once you get that last … little detail ironed out for me … she won't be any threat at all, will she?"

Cassidy swallowed uncomfortably. "That's … not a small detail. And the people who worked on it before me—"

"Didn't have half your intelligence," Harmon said. "Your meta ability is literally brain power." She puffed up a little, as he knew she would. She really didn't know people, including herself. She was absurdly susceptible to flattery, but then most people were. "Don't worry about Sienna Nealon. You take care of your part of this, and she won't be a problem." He lowered his voice, soothing her. "You finish this … and we won't ever have to worry about her again."

Sienna Nealon Will Return in

UNYIELDING

Out of the Box
Book 11

Coming November 22, 2016!

Author's Note

If you want to know immediately when future books become available, take sixty seconds and sign up for my NEW RELEASE EMAIL ALERTS by visiting my website at www.robertjcrane.com. I don't sell your information and I only send out emails when I have a new book out. The reason you should sign up for this is because I don't always set release dates, and even if you're following me on Facebook (robertJcrane (Author)) or Twitter (@robertJcrane), it's easy to miss my book announcements because...well, because social media is an imprecise thing.

Come join the discussion on my website: www.robertjcrane.com!

Cheers,
Robert J. Crane

ACKNOWLEDGMENTS

Editorial/Literary Janitorial duties performed by Sarah Barbour and Jeffrey Bryan. Final proofing was handled by Jo Evans. Any errors you see in the text, however, are the result of me rejecting changes. I owe a special apology to Jo for boobtacularly forgetting her incredible acknowledgments to the Sanctuary Series as I was thanking everybody in volume eight. Mea culpa, mea maxima culpa on that one, Jo.

The cover was once more designed masterfully by Karri Klawiter of Artbykarri.com.

The formatting was provided by nickbowmanediting.com. Well, by Nick, anyway.

Once more, thanks to my parents, my in-laws, my kids and my wife, for helping me keep things together.

Other Works by Robert J. Crane

World of Sanctuary
Epic Fantasy

Defender: The Sanctuary Series, Volume One
Avenger: The Sanctuary Series, Volume Two
Champion: The Sanctuary Series, Volume Three
Crusader: The Sanctuary Series, Volume Four
Sanctuary Tales, Volume One - A Short Story Collection
Thy Father's Shadow: The Sanctuary Series, Volume 4.5
Master: The Sanctuary Series, Volume Five
Fated in Darkness: The Sanctuary Series, Volume 5.5
Warlord: The Sanctuary Series, Volume Six
Heretic: The Sanctuary Series, Volume Seven
Legend: The Sanctuary Series, Volume Eight

A Haven in Ash: Ashes of Luukessia Trilogy, Volume One*
(Coming Early 2017!)

Ghosts of Sanctuary: The Revenants Series, Volume One*
(Coming 2018, at earliest.)

The Girl in the Box
and
Out of the Box
Contemporary Urban Fantasy

Alone: The Girl in the Box, Book 1
Untouched: The Girl in the Box, Book 2
Soulless: The Girl in the Box, Book 3
Family: The Girl in the Box, Book 4
Omega: The Girl in the Box, Book 5

Broken: The Girl in the Box, Book 6
Enemies: The Girl in the Box, Book 7
Legacy: The Girl in the Box, Book 8
Destiny: The Girl in the Box, Book 9
Power: The Girl in the Box, Book 10

Limitless: Out of the Box, Book 1
In the Wind: Out of the Box, Book 2
Ruthless: Out of the Box, Book 3
Grounded: Out of the Box, Book 4
Tormented: Out of the Box, Book 5
Vengeful: Out of the Box, Book 6
Sea Change: Out of the Box, Book 7
Painkiller: Out of the Box, Book 8
Masks: Out of the Box, Book 9
Prisoners: Out of the Box, Book 10
Unyielding: Out of the Box, Book 11* *(Coming November 22 2016!)*
Hollow: Out of the Box, Book 12* *(Coming January 2017!)*

Southern Watch
Contemporary Urban Fantasy

Called: Southern Watch, Book 1
Depths: Southern Watch, Book 2
Corrupted: Southern Watch, Book 3
Unearthed: Southern Watch, Book 4
Legion: Southern Watch, Book 5
Starling: Southern Watch, Book 6* *(Coming in Late 2016 – Tentatively)*

*Forthcoming

Made in the USA
Columbia, SC
06 September 2020